Have Portal. Will Travel.

Have Portal. Will Travel.

(Five original time travel short stories)

Cora Foerstner

Wood Sorrel Press, Redmond, WA

Contents

Introduction

My League of the Daring time travel, mystery series set in 1890s Los Angeles took an unexpected twist when I was writing *Miranda's Mystery*, the third book in the series.

I accidentally created the Time Travel University (TTU). Two of my characters wanted to leave their home and become time travelers. When I was writing, two characters wanting to leave seemed like a nice conflict for the novel.

When I finished *Miranda's Mystery*, I realized I had another time travel series sitting over in the corner of my mind staring at me and asking questions.

Are you going to write another time travel series? Does the new series have structure? A mission? Humorous and serious? Or is this simply a plot conflict in *Miranda's Mystery* that goes nowhere?

My strategy was to ignore the questions and the wannabe series that kept asking questions. But when something gets into my mind and hangs on, there's no ignoring it.

Why was I so hesitant?

The League of the Daring series characters fall into adventures and mysteries. The five characters do not have a serious agenda or any agenda at all. In those books, they learn about themselves and have fun romps together.

They use time travel as a tool to solve problems. In between the adventures, the characters lead everyday lives in their alternate history world where airships and time travel are real.

A series about time travelers with an agenda would be very different. Would this be a step into a very serious world? Did I want to go there?

To answer those two questions, I decided to write a few short stories about TTU and see what trouble my characters could get into. Also, I could figure out if I wanted to tackle another time travel series.

In *Miranda's Mystery*, Alroy and Lavinia plan to leave the 1890s and head over to the twenty-first century to attend TTU. When I started writing the short stories, I didn't know if TTU had a mission. In other words, I didn't take it seriously.

The obvious answers to why a university to teach people to time travel would be to help historians, scientists, anthropologists and others study the past. Of course, there were the old standbys—go back and kill Hitler. Or travel back in time to warn past generations they were messing up the future. Or time travelers could somehow change history to fix the future. Or they could send someone back to kill someone's mother.

Killing mommy? Yuck! Killing Hitler sounded noble—

one less monster, one less horrible world event. Killing someone's mother, well, that's something else.

So, to see if there was another road to take, I wrote these original short stories. Along the way, I found an idea that might become a worthwhile mission for my intrepid travelers.

If you've read the League of the Daring books, you've probably already guessed that Raymond, our favorite if somewhat unpredictable, Guardian, shows up in a couple stories to throw extra trouble into the mix. If you wonder what Alroy and Lavinia are up to at TTU, these are stories to satisfy you curiosity.

If you've never read the League of the Daring series but you like time travel stories, these stories were fun to write, and I hope entertaining reads.

Did I make a decision about writing the series? Nope! But I am toying with a few ideas.

The stories take place five years after *Miranda's Mystery*. Lavinia and Alroy are ready to take their final exams and become official time travelers. Their exams are time travel assignments they must complete to graduate. Of course, they encounter more problems and setbacks than anyone expected.

What could go wrong when the professors turn the time travel final into a scavenger hunt through time and space?

Read them and find out. Have fun.

Cora Foerstner, 2025

Author of *League of the Daring*

CORA FOERSTNER

Detours
and
Rescues

Beware of easy exams!

Detours & Rescues

Time Travel University, TTU, was founded on lofty ideas and steeped in secrecy. If that sounds completely ridiculous, remember that in the early twenty-first century, there were millions of people around the world who believed in outlandish and absurd conspiracy theories.

Time travel is impossible. Right?

Maybe . . . maybe not.

Moving on to factual information:

TTU was and is a private, by-invitation-only university. It also happened to be hidden.

Some students believed it was located in California. Others said New York, still others Europe. A few hypothesized the campus was hidden in the deep jungles along the Amazon River.

Lavinia, one of the first students to attend TTU, believed they were on a Hub somewhere in outer space.

No one knew.

Well, that wasn't entirely true. After several unfortunate events revealed the need to train time travelers, the older time travelers started TTU. They and the Guardians knew the location of the university.

Don't ask about the Guardians. That's another, no-no topic.

Students came from all around the world and from many different times. Most hailed from the late twentieth or twenty-first centuries. Others, like Lavinia and Alroy, came from the1890s Los Angeles.

Unfortunately, TTU, like most schools, had a pecking order. Students from the past were looked down upon. Why? Because the enlightened people of the twenty-first century believed those from the past weren't as knowledgeable or as intelligent.

Of course, that's another idiotic idea. The world is full of stupid, silly people and intelligent, practical people in every era. Recall the conspiracy theory people as well as Albert Einstein?

Five years have passed since the opening of TTU, and the first graduating class faces their final exams, which are by no stretch of the imagination typical examinations.

The morning of their first exam, Lavinia stood in front of the assignment board next to the cafeteria. She pressed her lips together until they felt numb. The eight-foot-by-four-foot digital board updated information regularly. Giant red letters across the top said TTU.

Announcements, class schedules, and most importantly, graduation exam schedules were written on what looked like parchment paper.

Everything at TTU was black and white, so parchment stood out like a charging bull. Bare white walls, tiles and carpeting, furniture, all were black and white. The monotony could drive a person crazy.

Lavinia never got used to it, but she learned to ignore the lack of stimuli by keeping her mind active.

Teresa, a short woman from Spain, stepped up beside her and studied the same list. She smelled like coffee and french toast. Coffee sounded good.

A second later, Teresa cursed in Spanish. At least Lavinia wasn't the only one disappointed with her assignment. The good thing about her assignment was that Alroy, one of her best friends since childhood, was on her team. For this test, teams had four people.

Seeing the other two names, her mind immediately reached the conclusion that whoever made the assignments wanted her and Alroy to fail.

Typical.

Everyone here, including the faculty, singled out people from other centuries. For two heartbeats, she considered consoling Teresa, but dismissed the idea.

She had her own problems. Samuel and Candice! Both were know-it-alls who weren't team players and messed up nearly every assignment they did. She didn't know how they'd survived this long.

There were three types of people who went to TTU. Time travelers, support personnel, and researchers.

Samuel and Candice were not time traveler material, but they were on that course.

Lavinia's only goal was to be a time traveler. If these two messed things up, she'd . . . she didn't know what she'd do, but she'd do something memorable.

She took a step away from the digital board. The board blinked, went black for a second, and then repopulated the data. That usually meant changes. Her heartbeats jumped, and her hope spiked as she turned back toward the assignment list.

Hope vanished. Her assignment hadn't changed.

Three other students groaned. Apparently, no one was happy about the assignments. She took a deep breath. Then she marched the short distance down the wide hallway to the cafeteria.

The white bare walls of the hallway were as antiseptic as always. Her new tennis shoes squeaked on the black and white tiles. She ignored the people who nodded or spoke as she hurried passed. Nearly five years living here and she still hated this building.

A few students stood in groups whispering and stopped to watch her. They'd seen the board and either felt sorry for her and Alroy, or they couldn't wait to see them fail.

The smell of toast, ham, and eggs filled the hall as she entered the dining area and stopped. The dining room would accommodate at least a hundred people. She glanced around at mostly empty tables, searching for Alroy among the sparse crowd.

Students tended to wear bright primary colors. Probably for the same reason she decorated her dorm room with anything colorful. Alroy, an outlier on the color scale, preferred browns. No brown anywhere.

TTU started with fifty-two students destined for time travel. They were down to thirty-one, which was as it should be. They needed support and researchers. The twelve or so people scattered around the room looked up as she entered.

"He's in the gym," Jackson called out, pointing left as if she could see the gym from the doorway.

Outside, the cloudless blue sky seemed unduly cheerful considering her plight. Even the warm temperature and the sunshine couldn't lift her spirit. One of the reasons she knew they were in space was because of the sunny skies and perfect seventy-degree weather that never deviated.

About thirty feet ahead, the gym, a large cinder block rectangle, fit in perfectly with the bland decor. This area was her favorite place to stroll and clear her mind. The wide cement walkway, intended for large numbers of students, was almost always empty. Flower beds of purple lily of the Nile, Santa Barbara daisy, iris, and sea lavender always cheered her.

Lavinia learned the names of all the flowers because they were the bright spots in a sea of neutral colors. This morning, she only gave them passing consideration as she hurried toward the gym. She flung open the door and found the massive room with its oak floors and basketball court empty.

Without pause, she turned left and headed toward the workout area. She spotted Alroy in the first training room dedicated to boxing, a vile sport that caused head injuries.

Alroy fought a serious conflict with one of the black punching bags. His damp tank top suggested he'd been at it for a while, punching the bag so hard it swung wide. Damp red hair cascaded over his forehead. His face glistened red.

They came from a time when everyone covered their bodies. Here shorts, tank tops, and flimsy fabric were the norm. At first she didn't know where to look. Faces were safe. After the first year, she was wearing tank tops and slacks. Two years in she braved shorts and swam in very skimpy bathing suits. Pedro, her old boyfriend still back in 1896, would have been shocked.

She shrugged. Change happened. They all had to get used to it.

When they'd arrived five years ago, Alroy'd been a thin sixteen-year-old with messy red hair and blue eyes that sparkled with mischief. Now, he was over six feet tall and muscular.

According to the female students, he was handsome in spite of his unruly red hair. To her, he was Alroy, one of her best friends since she could remember.

When he spotted her, he grabbed the punching bag and held the black swinging cylinder until it stopped. He scooped up the white towel on the bench beside him and wiped his face.

"You saw the list?" Alroy asked.

"What do we do?"

"I talked to Skyles. He said the assignments are part of the test. If we ask for a change, it'll be considered a failure. We have to deal with their nonsense."

She glanced around and tried to ignore her frustration. This room always stank. Something about the men's body odor in this room repulsed her.

"So, we're screwed." Oh, yeah, she also used slang.

Funny, considering Alroy's nineteenth-century slang, "corker," slang for "jolly good," always annoyed her. Since coming here, she'd stepped into secular vocabulary with ease.

Alroy walked over to the white basket in the corner and tossed in his towel.

"You wanna punch things for a while?"

She chuckled. "No. I'd like to know where we're going."

"That is the question. There's a positive. All the exams are recorded. If Samuel and Candice do anything stupid, maybe it won't affect us."

"Let's hope they put one of us in charge."

Alroy shook his head and the light from the window accented his right eye. Someone definitely punched him in the face, recently. The skin around his eye was red and puffy.

"Not going to happen," Alroy said. "If they put us with people who are difficult to work with, they aren't going to put us in charge."

"Your eye?"

"Yeah. I checked the board early and said something slightly derogatory about Samuel and Candice. He was standing behind me."

She stared at him. Some part of her wanted to punch him in the other eye. She took a couple seconds to debate the advantages and disadvantages of following through on her instinct.

"Okay, I made it worse. But they have to get along with us too, or they'll fail." He pointed to his chin. "Go ahead. Hit me right here."

She crossed her arms and took a deep breath. "I don't resort to violence to solve problems."

He grinned, his blue eyes squinting. "Is that so? I remember—"

"Shut up."

They both chuckled.

Two hours later, Lavinia and Alroy sat in Dr. Lancaster's classroom with the other students scheduled for the first test. Samuel and Candice sat on the other side of the room. If Candice's look of glaring hatred was any indication, she and Alroy were in a world of trouble.

All their class sizes were smallish, twelve students seemed to be the limit. Each classroom had twelve large mahogany desks with comfortable chairs. Lavinia loved the roomy desks, because she could spread out books and take notes. The learning environment suited her.

Since they studied history, culture, lore, anthropology, and other social sciences, Alroy took to this curriculum immediately. Lavinia grew used to it.

Science had been her love in 1890. Coming to the twenty-first century changed her in ways she hadn't foreseen. Science had advanced so much she was behind.

Professor Zenn tutored her in science and its history. It was easy to catch up on the new discoveries. Studying advanced science and mathematics took longer.

Someday she'd catch up. Her plan then was to go to a regular university for a degree in physics.

At home, Lavinia always thought her mixed race as a problem to be overcome. Here in the future, she discovered most people didn't care about her white father and black mother.

However, TTU wasn't completely progressive. Being from 1890 moved them into the second-class-citizen category. They were from the past and had to be uneducated and ignorant. That bias turned out to be a blessing.

The students from other eras banded together and helped each other. They were determined to become better than the twenty-first-century students.

When they first arrived, Samuel led the charge to get everyone from the past disqualified from time travel. He claimed they didn't have the mental capacity for the rigors of time travel. Of course, she and Alroy got together with the other seven students and formed the Past Travelers Club to help each other and prove Samuel wrong.

That put all of them on his and later on Candice's bad sides. The fact that all the Past Travelers did well on everything didn't help.

Lavinia's wristwatch computer vibrated. The screen lit up with a message from Bella, the AI teacher in their computer system.

No one is going to a location or time that they have studied. The goal is to see how you handle the unknown.

Being in league with Bella was a little bit of a cheat, but no one ever told them they couldn't use her help. That was one of the first things she and Alroy taught their Past Travelers Club. Two rows over, Jenifer looked at her watch screen and glanced back at Lavinia, who nodded. No matter what happened, their group would stick together.

Alroy hurried into the room, sliding into his seat across from her just as Professor Lancaster walked into the room. Professor Lancaster was Lavinia's favorite teacher. Every class she dressed in a costume from a different time period and different profession.

Today, she looked like someone from an old black and white movie, an archaeologist with tan pants, shirts, boots, and even a pith helmet.

"What's today's costume?" Lancaster took off her pith helmet and shook out her long brown hair, letting the curls free.

"Archaeologist," someone in the back shouted.

"Correct. Today, each group is traveling back to an unfamiliar time period and place. You will find items we have hidden there. You will go, retrieve the items, and return. Each of you will be given a specific item to recover. I'll tell you this up front. Your success will depend on working together. There are possible dangers with each task. Remember your training. Questions?"

"Can we use our translators?" Jane asked.

"Of course."

"What is one thing you aren't telling us?" Alroy asked.

Professor Lancaster grinned. Under normal circumstances, her face looked passive and expressionless, but when she smiled, her face lit up and mischief danced in her eyes.

"Always looking for an angle, Alroy."

"Yes, ma'am."

"Time. You are being timed. You aren't sightseeing. You're on the clock."

"Does that mean taking too long could be a fail?"

"Bingo!" She pointed to Alroy. "Now, go see Beth and Homer. They have prepared your clothes. Then meet Professor Skyles at the Station."

Beth and Homer started the program with Lavinia and Alroy. After three time travel assignments, they requested to be changed to support. They hated stepping into portals and PODs terrified them.

They did an amazing job of researching clothing, luggage, accessories, maps, customs, and more. Lavinia admired the research and enthusiasm they put into their work.

When she and Alroy arrived, there was a line. Samuel and Candice stood four people in front of them. So far they hadn't spoken, but at some point they had to make a plan and work together. For now, Lavinia ignored them as they inched their way forward.

Homer handed Samuel a somewhat modern-looking suit and dress shoes. So they weren't going far back. From where she stood the fabric and style looked like the recent past.

Beth smiled when Lavinia stepped up. "As per your usual." She handed Lavinia a suit, men's dress shoes, a hat and a short cut wig.

"Where are we going," Lavinia whispered.

"Bogotá, capital of Colombia."

Lavinia had to lean in to hear her.

"South America. 1970. Don't let on that you know."

Professor Skyles waited for them at the door to the

Station. Back in Los Angeles in 1890, time travelers used Hubs, not Stations.

Basically they were the same thing. The only difference was that travelers entered a Hub through a portal and went to an unknown location in outer space. They entered and left through a portal in Los Angeles.

Her experiences were part of the reason Lavinia knew that, although their university looked like it was on earth, it wasn't. She gave up trying to convince the other students of this fact because they thought she was crazy. The entire university was a Hub.

The Station was a room filled with PODs, time travel vehicles that held six people, supplies, sleeping chairs, computers, and all the accommodations they needed to travel to another time and place. They took their hotel with them.

The POD had stealth technology that could blend into any environment. Usually they were used for longer trips, or for dangerous trips where a hiding place or quick escape for several people might be necessary.

Lavinia had the distinct impression they were using the PODs for safety. Professor Skyles handed Lavinia a small envelope and checked her name off his list.

"POD five," he said, as he handed Alroy his envelope.

The Station had the usual black and white floor, concrete because there was a team of engineers and mechanics who worked on the PODs and kept all the equipment they needed in perfect order.

Today, there wasn't much going on. Jeffrey, one of the mechanics Alroy knew, waited for them by POD five.

He handed Alroy the equipment list. "Your team

members are inside." He glanced around before whispering. "They aren't very nice. Be careful."

"We'll be fine."

When they entered the POD, Samuel sat in the pilot's seat, and Candice sat next to him. Neither one had changed into their time period clothes. Lavinia stepped behind the privacy screen and changed into her brown suit, which fit her perfectly, even the shoes were comfortable.

Since she and her best friend Zella had started time traveling, they chose to dress like men. No matter where they went, no one paid attention to men. Women got noticed. She continued the custom here.

After she'd changed, she came out to see Alroy dressed and going through the equipment checklist. The POD wasn't large, but somehow it felt roomy. Comfortable chairs were attached to the floor. Each chair converted to a bed.

Alroy stood by the tall cabinets, which were filled with supplies. This was Lavinia's favorite mode of travel. It was so much nicer than stepping through a portal and just appearing in open space and shocking people.

So far, Samuel and Candice hadn't said a word. When Alroy grabbed the first aid kit and started for the door, Samuel spoke.

"Where you going? I'm ready to go."

"The first aid kit isn't complete. Whoever used it last didn't restock it. I'll be right back."

"Then I'll leave without you."

"Leaving a crew member behind. That should get you a passing grade." Alroy opened the door.

"No one checks the equipment list. Get back in here."

"I check the equipment list." Alroy stepped outside.

Lavinia sat in the swivel chair behind Candice. "When Alroy gets back we should look at each of our quests and make a plan."

Samuel turned his chair so he faced her. His dark hair was slicked back and looked greasy. If he had a more pleasant personality, his handsome face and broad shoulders might have been attractive.

"I heard about your little gang back in the Wild West. League of the Daring, right? A stupid childish name. We aren't playing games here. Candice and I will get our artifacts and come back to the POD. If you and the League of the Daring boy are late, we'll leave you behind."

He wanted to provoke her, and she wasn't going to play his game. "That's your choice, but if we work together, we can do this quickly."

"We don't give a shit what you think," Candice said in her squeaky voice. Her long blond hair had natural curls that always seemed to fall perfectly in place to frame her cute face and little button nose.

The door opened and Alroy stepped inside with a new first aid kit.

"All set." He glanced at Lavinia. "What's up? Something happen while I was gone?"

"Nothing happened," Candice said. "We just set the rules. You and your girlfriend are on your own. Sam and I will get our loot and come back here. If you don't hurry, we'll leave you. Got it?"

"You agreed to this?" Alroy asked.

Lavinia shook her head. "Of course not. It's a stupid idea."

"Nonnegotiable," Samuel said.

Alroy placed the first aid kit in the closet and locked the door. "For the record, I don't agree with this plan. It's your responsibility." He moved forward and stood behind Samuel as he keyed in their destination.

"Get back," Samuel shouted.

"You've put in the wrong coordinates." Alroy pointed to the screen.

"You want me to punch you again?"

"Fine. Let's see where you're taking us."

While they bantered, Candice looked at the screen's coordinates and compared that to the papers in front of her.

"Sam—"

Samuel pushed the green button on the black dashboard just as Alroy sat in his chair and started to buckle his seat belt. The whining sound of the start-up drowned out Candice's words.

The POD shook oddly and jolted to a stop.

Lavinia checked the computer screen to her right. The landscape outside the POD looked like a jungle or perhaps a rain forest, tall trees, sunlight filtering through the foliage, and two brown monkeys staring at them as if they could see the POD. She spotted a river in the distance and two huts with grass roofs about thirty feet away.

In front of her, Samuel and Candice stared out their large window. Both of them leaned forward.

"I was just saying. You did the coordinates wrong," Candice said. "Here. I'll do it."

Across from Lavinia, Alroy grinned like the Cheshire Cat.

Candice cleared the coordinates and reentered them. Lavinia leaned forward to tell Candice she needed to adjust the coordinates for their current location.

As she pointed toward the controls, Samuel slapped her hand away. Before Lavinia could speak, he hit the green button again. The POD shook for at least twenty seconds, which was unusual. POD travel was almost instantaneous. Finally, they landed again.

Alroy hung his head to hide his wide grin. He had a knack for putting on an attitude that made things worse.

"Alroy," Lavinia shouted. "Look."

She held up her computer screen. The POD sat high on a mountain range, in the clouds. The sensation the POD was teetering wasn't imaginary.

Alroy unbuckled his seat belt. "Get up you two. Now."

"No," Candice said. "We can do this."

"Do you know where we are?" Lavinia asked, standing and moving forward.

"Yes," Samuel said. "I do. Sit down. I've got this."

She glanced at Alroy.

"I say, let them dig their own grave," Alroy said and pointed to her chair.

She sat, thinking this was their grave too. Finally she said, "You do know that the coordinates are wrong, don't you?"

"No, they aren't. I have them right here." Candice waved the paper.

Samuel continued to stare out the window. "We are somewhere in the mountains. High. The Andes?" He spoke as if he were talking to himself.

Alroy was enjoying the fiasco. Lavinia was not.

Trying as hard as she could to control her voice to sound normal and not yell, she spoke.

"The coordinates and our destination were set from the Station to Bogotá. When you sent us somewhere else, we needed to adjust the coordinates. Now we need to adjust them again."

By the end of that speech, her voice had gone up a couple of octaves.

"If you're so smart, you do it," Candice said.

Alroy stood. "Candice, I think Samuel is in shock. You need to help him up and get him into my chair."

She crossed her arms and pushed her lower lip out. "You do it."

"No," Samuel shouted. "I've got it."

The POD teetered and, as if in slow motion, it slid downward. Samuel frantically punched in new coordinates. Alroy plopped down in his chair and buckled his seat belt. He glanced at Lavinia as the POD continued its bumpy, shaking downward speed.

The sound of metal scraping rock didn't ease her nerves. From the view window Lavinia watched rocks and debris flying around them. The POD bounced drastically.

She imagined the POD damaged and destroyed . . . them along with it.

The whine came first, and then the shaking as they landed somewhere else.

Lavinia jumped up and went to the control panel and looked out the large window. They were in the middle of a desert. It didn't look like a California desert, but more like a Middle Eastern desert.

"We've seen the jungle, the top of the Andes, and now a desert. Anyplace else you want to go before we return to the Station and get kicked out of the program?" This time she didn't try to hide her anger.

"Bella," Alroy said. "Where are we?"

Bella's hologram appeared beside Alroy. She looked like a teenager. She wore shorts and had pink hair pulled back in a ponytail. She grinned as if she were enjoying Samuel's antics.

"You are in Saudi Arabia, 1153 BCE. I'd say you are officially off track."

Alroy yanked Samuel out of his chair and shoved him toward one of the other empty chairs. He glared at Candice.

"Get up." As she stood, he pointed to the copilot seat. "Lavinia. Bella, please recalculate the coordinates for us."

The new coordinates showed up on Lavinia and Alroy's personal computers. As was their custom, Lavinia read the coordinates, Alroy punched them in, and Lavinia double-checked them. Within seconds, they landed near a tan adobe wall.

In front of them, the *Plaza de Bolívar* spread out, a sweeping plaza filled with people dressed in mid-twentieth century clothes. Women wore dresses and heels. They men all wore suits.

Some people milled about while others walked past their POD. Lampposts uniformly placed encircled the large plaza, and in the center of the massive square a statue of Simón Bolívar.

"Those large buildings are the municipal buildings. The ornate building with the two towers is the Cathedral of Bogotá," Lavinia said.

"How do you know that?" Candice asked.

Lavinia almost said because I read, but considering how badly they performed with the coordinates, she softened her answer.

"I did a report in high school. There's a rich history here."

"We don't care," Samuel said. "Get your artifact and get back here or we leave without you. And, Lavinia, you look stupid."

Samuel practically shoved Candice out of the POD. Neither of them had changed their clothes. She and Alroy opened their envelopes.

Lavinia read hers aloud. "At the top of the tower behind a woven basket, bring back the *tinto*." She grinned. "I'm getting coffee. You?"

"A copy of *Don Quixote*. Same tower. I have to barter the price down."

Lavinia stood. "Then I shall barter as well. We need Colombian *pesos*."

Alroy reached into his pocket and pulled out a wad of bills. "If there's leftover, I'll buy you something."

They stepped outside into the chilly afternoon. Dark clouds gathered in the sky. In the plaza, people dressed more formal. Some men even sported hats. Most of the women wore long coats, so she couldn't tell much about the dresses. Platform shoes and stockings abounded, not something the twenty-first century girls wore.

Hundreds of gray and some white pigeons roamed in the plaza, flying away if people got too near.

She and Alroy strolled across the plaza toward the church. Lavinia caught a whiff of meat and glanced around. A man stood beside a cart with a glass top that covered crescent-shaped pastries. From the smell, she figured they were savory. His sign said *Empanadas*.

She'd read about meat, rice, and vegetables filling the pastries. They had something similar in Los Angeles. Pedro's mother made them once a week or so.

The air felt light as if oxygen were scarce. Bogotá sat on a plateau high in the Andes. She forced herself to take deep breaths.

"Which tower?" Alroy asked.

She grinned. "My guess, the one with the Curio Shop sign."

Lavinia had to hurry to keep up with Alroy's long strides. When they stepped into the shop, the musty smell of old books and dust tickled her nose. She willed herself not to sneeze.

An older priest sat behind a long counter, reading a thin leather-bound book. His black robes seemed to swallow his slim frame. He glanced at them with milky eyes and a wide smile. His hands shook as he set his book aside.

"Are you looking for something specific?" he asked.

Of course he spoke Spanish, but they heard in perfect English. Their translators also turned their English into Spanish.

"Don Quixote."

The old priest chuckled. "Everyone's favorite. I have new ones here." He pointed to the shelf behind them.

"I prefer an old copy. Something to impress my friends."

He pointed up. "The older books are up."

If the entry was musty and dusty, the extremely narrow staircase hadn't been dusted in centuries. She swore dust billowed up as they climbed the steps. Only a few steps up, Lavinia sneezed.

"Bless you," the old man called out.

They didn't bother sightseeing on the way up, they went directly to the top, with Lavinia sneezing and covering her face with her arm. She found the woven basket immediately and the bag of Colombian coffee.

Alroy's task proved a little more challenging. He found three copies of *Don Quixote*, one had Professor Skyles' signature on the inside. Bingo!

Alroy bartered the price down to almost half, and Lavinia's small bag of coffee beans confused the priest so much, he gave it to her as a gift. On their way back to the POD, they bought four *empanadas* to share with Samuel and Candice.

When they arrived, the POD was empty. They heated water and made tea. They decided not to wait for their partners and ate their *empanadas* with tea. While Alroy debated aloud the possibility of eating the second *empanada*, Lavinia grew a little concerned that Samuel and Candice hadn't returned.

"They're fine," Alroy said.

"In light of our multiple attempts to get here, and the

fact they didn't dress for the occasion, I think we should check on them."

Alroy sat in the pilot's chair with his legs resting on the control console as he gazed out over the plaza. "I don't really want to help them, but we shouldn't be idiots just because they are. Send them a message."

"I just did."

"They might not answer."

Lavinia ate the second *empanada* while she monitored her personal computer for a message. None came.

"Bella," Alroy said. "Where are Samuel and Candice?"

Bella's hologram appeared next to the console. "I suspect they are in police custody. Their pocket computers have been confiscated. Right now, it is at a temporary police station next to the cathedral."

"Any idea why they are arrested?" Lavinia asked.

"Theft."

Lavinia stood up. "Let's go."

"Are we going to break them out of jail?"

"I don't know. We'll go there and see what happens. We need to get them and their equipment. Bella, can you make us something official-looking so we can get them released?"

The 3D printer turned on. "I'm printing DAS badges for you. Administrative Department of Security."

"That sounds like—"

"Secret Service," Lavinia said.

"Yes," Bella said. "Get there quickly, get them and their devices, and get out. I'm sure there are real DAS agents on their way."

DAS badges in their pockets, they hurried across the

plaza, and into an office that was about twelve feet wide by twenty feet. Back behind the counter was a cage that looked more primitive than the jail cells in 1890.

A police officer, who was clearly sleeping when they entered the building, jumped up and straightened his uniform. He had the largest nose Lavinia had ever seen and blue eyes. He cleared his throat.

"May I help you?"

Samuel and Candice sat side by side in the cell and didn't bother to look up when they entered. Lavinia guessed they were in shock.

She and Alroy took their badges out at once and flipped them open. Juan wore a name tag on his shirt.

"Good work, Officer Juan," Lavinia said. "We've had our eye on those two for years."

The police officer glanced back. "Spies? CIA?"

Lavinia nodded.

"Keep this under your hat." She didn't know how that translated into Spanish, but she didn't care. She wanted to get out of here quickly. "Can't tell anyone. This is top secret. You'll probably get an commendation."

The officer straightened and nodded. Samuel and Candice finally noticed them.

"Alroy, Lavinia," Candice said.

The officer squinted. "They know you?"

Alroy stepped around the counter and stood close to the officer.

"Those two are dangerous. They've killed several people. Sure, they know us. We've been chasing them across the country. We need their belongings, and we'll take them now."

Juan glanced at the cell. "She looks so innocent and pretty."

"She is more dangerous than he is." Lavinia took the folded papers from her pocket and handed them to Juan. "I need your signature and their belongings."

He glanced at the paperwork. He handed the cell keys to Alroy, and signed the papers. He gave Lavinia a brown cloth bag. She glanced inside. There was only one personal computer. She held it up.

"There should be another one of these."

Juan started like a kid caught with his hand in the candy jar. He hurried to his desk and pulled the other one from the top drawer.

"I kept it because it kept making noise and oscillating." He handed it to her.

Alroy led Samuel and Candice out of the cell and handcuffed them. Another minute for pleasantries, and they were out onto the plaza. As they reached the Bolívar statue, Lavinia noticed two men walking into the police station.

"Hurry," Lavinia said. "I think the real agents just went into the police station. Bella, open the POD door, now."

She quickened her pace as she guided Candice toward the POD.

Behind them someone shouted, "Stop. Stop. Down, everyone."

A shot rang out.

Candice leaped forward and stumbled. She scraped her face across the plaza's bricks. Lavinia yanked her upright.

"Keep running," Lavinia urged her.

Around them people ran for cover. Others shouted and pointed toward them.

Lavinia dragged Candice, who fought her each step of the way. Alroy shoved Samuel forward. Then he grabbed Candice's other arm. Together they raced forward.

Two more shots rang out. A bullet hit the brick plaza to Lavinia's right. A few feet ahead, the door to the POD stood open.

"Run," Alroy shouted to Samuel who seemed to be losing steam.

When Samuel slowed instead of picking up speed, Alroy released Candice. She ran in earnest now. He grabbed Samuel, slinging him toward the POD.

Alroy pushed Samuel forward as they raced for the POD. Lavinia shoved Candice into the POD and followed her. Samuel stumbled through the door as if he'd been shoved hard.

Last in, Alroy closed the door. Lavinia bent over breathing hard, trying to catch her breath. She moved to the observation window. The two DAS agents searched the area around the pod. She clicked on the listening device.

"I swear I saw them run into this alcove."

The taller of the two men shoved his gun into its holster.

"I saw it too. They had help. Let's blame everything on Juan. He's the one who let them walk away."

After walking around the area for several more seconds, the two agents strolled toward the police station.

Lavinia sank into the copilot's seat and swiveled

around to face Samuel and Candice who had collapsed into the extra seats.

"Are you going to tell the teachers what happened?" Candice asked.

"Candice, the examinations are recorded. They know everything we have said and done."

"You finished your quest?" Samuel looked away when Lavinia met his gaze.

Alroy went to the cabinet and pulled out the first aid kit and tossed it to Samuel.

"Yes, we finished our quest. Help Candice with her face," Alroy said.

To Lavinia's surprise, Samuel opened the first aid kit and moved closer to Candice.

Alroy tossed the bag with their devices and the gold statue of a man with an elaborate headdress and an erect penis onto the chair next to them.

"How did you steal a gold statue? I'm sure that's not what you were supposed to retrieve."

Candice licked her lips. "We went into the gold museum. I think we were supposed to go to the gift shop, but . . . ."

She glanced at Samuel.

"We made a mistake. He broke the glass and took it. I think we took three steps before the guards stopped us."

Lavinia kept the *how could you be so stupid* comment to herself.

"We need to get out of here," she said instead.

She inputted the code as Alroy buckled himself into the pilot's chair.

They returned to TTU to be greeted by stern-faced

teachers and grinning students. In a small community like this one, nothing stayed a secret. Samuel and Candice were reassigned to support. She and Alroy passed the first test. Professor Skyles said they deserved extra credit for fast thinking.

He also pointed out that in 1970, an international scandal between the CIA and the Colombian government strained relationships for a couple of years. The American Embassy was on high alert for several months while they tried to figure out if their people stole a gold statue and infiltrated DAS.

That night Candice came to Lavinia's room and discovered the world of color and comfort could be found by currying favor with Bella. She also thanked Lavinia for saving her and admitted that she was thankful to be moved to support. She hated time travel and only did it for Samuel.

Author of *League of the Daring*
CORA FOERSTNER
A Visit to the Globe!
Beware the dodger in merry England!

A Visit to the Globe

Alroy lay on the grass, his arms folded so his head rested in his hands. He gazed at the rose garden. As far as beauty went, the roses were nearly perfect, and a riot of pink, white, red, yellow, and some dark ones that looked nearly black.

If Lavinia were here, she could tell him their names. Since they arrived at the Time Travel University, she'd taken an unusual interest in the grounds and particularly the flowers.

In most aspects, the school was so drab it felt as if the administration delighted in starkness and blandness. So he understood her love of color and being out here in nature.

He admitted he came here to enjoy the outdoors and to think. The gentle breeze carried the aroma of roses to him. In spite of their beauty, he preferred the roses in 1890. Sure they weren't as big or as perfectly shaped, but the fragrance was stronger. At home, all it took was a slight breeze for their aroma to fill the air and the house.

He took a deep breath and admitted to himself that he was homesick and a little tired of being cooped up here. Sometimes he envied Zella, his sister, Toby, and Pedro. They chose to stay in 1890 Los Angeles. They had the freedom he longed for himself. On days like this he wondered if he'd made a mistake to follow the time travel path.

Every day this week the students ready to graduate took a time travel test. He and Lavinia had passed the first test. If they hadn't been paired with two people who didn't have the aptitude for time travel, that test would have been easy. Exam number two would take place in an hour and a half.

That was the other reason he was here, lying on the damp grass, staring and thinking. Three weeks ago, Mr. Skyles asked everyone to choose two places in history they would like to visit. Sounded simple, but the man has a tendency to make simple things complex.

Lavinia and the other members of the Past Travelers Club ignored Alroy when he cautioned them to expect the worst. They all thought they were going to get a chance to go to their first or second choices. He hoped that was true.

He had an uneasy feeling that Mr. Skyles was going to mix things up and send different people to places the other students wanted to go. Which probably wouldn't be bad, but Robert Greyson loved war.

Closing his eyes, he thought of all the terrible places he didn't want to be. The Civil War and Napoleon's wars with Europe. Since coming here, he'd studied World War

I, World War II, Vietnam, the Middle East. There were more. He couldn't think of them all.

It seemed to him humanity had gone crazy. In 1890, they'd worried about crime, getting the most recent technology, and making the world better. Yes, he was definitely homesick. Only now he knew that in a few short years, his family and friends would face the first World War.

He was glad he didn't have to experience those things, but he knew his family and friends would. That ate at him.

Alroy loved adventure, but not danger. Seeing new places, meeting new people, helping people. Those were his kinds of adventures. Sure, he'd been in dangerous situations, but he didn't know ahead of time that they were going to be dangerous.

When Skyles gave the assignment, Alroy chose visiting the opening of the Eiffel tower in 1889 and The Chicago World's Fair in 1893. These were two things he'd only read about. Eventually, he could go there, but not with Zella and the others.

Behind him he heard Lavinia and Teresa talking and laughing as they came toward him. He stood up and dusted the grass off his pants. Enough feeling sorry for himself.

"Alroy," Teresa called out. "Are you ready for our next exam?"

"The schedule is posted?" He walked toward them and knew from their smiles that they were pleased with the groupings.

"Yes," Lavinia called out.

He hurried up the cement path to meet them. Lavinia's brown eyes sparkled with amusement. She had the most perfect bronze skin and black shiny hair that fell to her shoulders.

Here she found acceptance. No one cared about race and gender. There were some good things about the future, and more accepting people was a plus.

Lavinia put her arm through his, and Teresa took his other arm. As silly as it sounded, he liked walking arm and arm with two pretty girls.

It reminded him of being home, where men offered their arms to women, or in this case two. Teresa was from Spain in 1890 something, which was probably part of the reason they got along so well.

"Tell me," he said, smiling and leaving behind his negative thoughts.

"We don't know the assignments yet," Lavinia said. "But you, Teresa, Richard, and I are grouped together."

He smiled in earnest. "Wonderful. Four sensible people, that should be helpful. Any hints about what we are doing."

"Observation," Teresa said.

"Not a scavenger hunt then?"

"I wouldn't rule that out. We probably have to have some sort of proof for our reports."

"Ah, great. They couldn't just let us go have fun." Alroy frowned.

His sister loved writing and research. She would have made a perfect time traveler, but she wanted to stay in their time period and become a reporter. Alroy hated writing. He hadn't counted on that aspect of time travel.

Trying to be inconspicuous, he leaned closer to Teresa who smelled like jasmine this morning.

"You smell like jasmine," Alroy said.

Teresa actually blushed.

"I told you," Lavinia said.

"What?"

"Her mother sent her a scented lotion. She insisted it didn't smell like jasmine."

"Well, it does. It's lovely and reminds me of home," Alroy said.

Both girls chuckled.

"I told her you'd like it because your house is surrounded by jasmine."

It was his turn to blush because he wondered if Teresa wore the lotion for him. He hoped not because he'd had two girlfriends since he started here. When they didn't last, things got awkward, and not just between him and the girls, but their friends too. He promised himself not to get involved with anyone else.

"Where to?" he asked.

"Professor Skyles' classroom."

They stepped into the teaching building. Teachers had offices on the ground floor. Classrooms were on the second floor. This building, like all the buildings, was almost unbearably stark. The dorm rooms were a different matter. Students decorated to excess, probably because white walls became tedious very quickly.

They headed up to room 12, Professor Skyles' classroom with expansive desks, comfortable chairs, and white walls. The floors were some sort of black and white tiles.

Obviously, the decor was compliments of the Guardians who built the university.

This room broke the black-and-white theme of the university. Skyles put paintings on the walls. His discipline? History, of course. He loved the Renaissance, especially the English Renaissance.

Several sketches and paintings of the Globe dotted the walls. On one wall he'd hung paintings of Johnson, Shakespeare, Christopher Marlowe, da Vinci, Michelangelo, Copernicus, and Galileo. Alroy thought Machiavelli's eyes and tight little smile made him look deceptive and unreliable.

They took seats in the front row where Richard waited for them. Skyles stood in the front of the room writing on the white board. When he stepped sideways, Alroy saw a list of Shakespeare's plays with dates beside the titles. Skyles looked around and grinned.

He rubbed his hands together and smiled. "We are all here. Let's get started. Today, you are all going to London to see a Shakespearean play. Depending on the play, some of you will be going to the Globe Theatre and others to the Blackfriars Theatre."

He threw folded-up papers into a brown basket that looked as if it had been handmade with reeds. Knowing the professor, it probably was. He moved around to each group and one person chose a folded paper. Skyles shook the basket and held it out for Teresa to pick.

When she opened it, she turned to the others and whispered, *"Julius Caesar* at the Globe."

Alroy met her gaze as she smiled at him. Her blue eyes

seemed bluer than usual and dark wavy hair framed her face. She blushed and looked away.

He exhaled and knew he'd have to do something about this. Why? They'd been friends for years, and she'd never acted this way before. Lavinia raised her eyebrows at him as if expecting him to say something. He didn't.

Skyles called out names of someone from each group, including Alroy.

"If I called your name, you are the leader of your group. That means you are in charge of setting up your POD, setting the destination, and making sure everyone gets back safely. Every group is going to a different time. Your group report is due on my desk by noon Wednesday. Any questions?"

Their next stop was costumes, where those in charge of the group POD got their clothes first. At equipment, Alroy picked up everything he needed to get the POD ready, and a PEB, personal escape button, or EB as everyone except for the staff called it.

The tiny button fit into the palm of his hand. If anything happened, pressing the EB would bring the person back to the school. He had a feeling that using this would be a failing grade. What the others didn't know was that Lavinia and Alroy had their own personal EB. Lavinia's looked like a white eraser. Alroy's was a small bronze compass.

By the time Alroy got to the POD, he had a tick in his eyelid. He tried to ignore the erratic movement, told himself he wasn't nervous, but the constant movement around his eye distracted him. This was like any other assignment.

Only it wasn't. This reminded him of the League of the Daring's training. He'd gotten drunk and ruined the outing. Lavinia was the only one who knew he was an alcoholic. It wasn't something he talked about or wanted to remember.

Happy to be in the POD alone, he meticulously rechecked the information he'd inputted into the computer. London. 1602. Skyles' neat handwriting said the location would park them in an alley three blocks from the Globe Theatre.

He rechecked the map and confirmed the landing spot coordinates. Muttering aloud, he walked himself through the plan. Leave the POD in the alley, a less populated area. Walk east three blocks. Watch the *Julius Caesar* performance. Pray I see William Shakespeare. Look around for an hour. Back to the POD. Then back to the school.

His hand shook as he checked the destination, time of arrival, and date one last time.

He leaned back and sank into the comfort of the POD chair and grinned, congratulating himself. This was going to be a fantastic trip.

Every POD could hold six travelers, and was equipped with chairs that converted into beds, food, equipment, and every imaginable supply they might need.

PODs blended into the environment and couldn't be seen. Basically, they were invisible.

"Bella. I'm ready."

Bella's hologram appeared next to him.

"I'll tell the others you're ready." Bella's hologram vanished.

He sighed. POD travel was not his favorite method.

More things could go wrong, like inputting the wrong time or date or location, which he did once, and they wound up in a desolate future he never wanted to return to again.

Teresa was the first one in and took the seat next to him. Her eyes shone with excitement. At least he hoped it was excitement.

"I can't wait," she said. "London. Shakespeare. The Globe. *Julius Caesar.*"

Lavinia and Richard trooped in and took their seats. Even the girls were dressed as men. Alroy didn't usually pay much attention to their costumes. Today he wore a brown linen doublet with a stiff lacy collar and matching lace on his sleeves. The lace was scratching his neck.

Worse than the lace was his codpiece. He was glad he didn't have a full-length mirror. His hat was black and sort of like a flat hat. He also had a black cape that went to his knees. The others were dressed similarly and just as uncomfortable as he was.

He placed his leather pouch on his belt, and Lavinia informed him he should wear it on the inside of his doublet. He ignored her.

"Seat belts?" When everyone answered, he began the countdown."Ready, three, two, one."

He pushed the "Take Off" button, which was just a red button. The POD made a whining noise. The pressure from the POD pushed them all back in their chairs. The first time he traveled in a POD, he had shouted "damnation," and Lavinia shouted "holy cow."

This time, they all knew what to expect, and the POD seemed quiet. When they landed, everyone undid their seatbelts and switched on their computers. Teresa and Lavinia used the cameras to check the area, making sure it was safe to exit unnoticed. Richard rechecked the map, located the Globe, and leaned toward Alroy.

That's when Alroy whiffed his whiskey breath. "You've been drinking. You said you quit. Where'd you get it?"

Richard yanked his arm away. "Shut up."

"Everyone has water and snacks," Lavinia called out. "Check your ETs. Make sure they are secure"

Alroy glared at Richard. A feeling of *déjà vu* swept over him. Only he'd been the one who was drunk on a mission. He pushed the memory away.

"This side of the POD is clear," Teresa said.

"So is mine," Lavinia said.

"Let's go." Alroy stood.

Teresa and Lavinia exited. Alroy stepped next to Richard. "Stay next to me."

"No."

"I'm the leader. I can call everyone back and return to the TTU."

Richard stepped back. "You'd do that just to spite me?"

"No. You're a risk. You're drunk. You could get us hurt or in trouble. I don't want a repeat of my first exam."

Richard glared at him for a few seconds. "I can drink all I want."

Alroy grabbed his arm. "Yeah, you can, but not when we are time traveling and need our wits about us."

They stepped out of the POD. Alroy took a deep breath and coughed, choking on air that smelled like a latrine.

"What did you expect?" Lavinia asked. "Lead the way."

Alroy glanced back, making sure the POD was invisible. A cacophony of distant voices came from the street ahead. He glanced at the map he'd sketched on his hand, and took off in the direction of the Globe.

As he walked out of the alley, the smell of unbathed bodies, burnt meat, and excrement increased. Occasionally someone passed who reeked of perfume. Perfume mixed with all the raw smells didn't set well on his stomach.

The crowd was larger than he expected. Street vendors hawking their wares, mostly food and drink. Most of the people were dirty, and their clothes untidy. A few well dressed people walked in the direction of the Globe. Alroy had to force himself not to hold his nose, everyone from poor to wealthy reeked.

When Richard slowed or veered off, Alroy pulled him next to him and reminded him to stay close. This wasn't going to be the day he'd planned.

Despite the noise and smells Alroy glanced around like a tourist seeing a city for the first time. Being here was like stepping into a play or watching a photograph come to life. The experience was awe-inspiring and overwhelming. Noise, costumes, smells, both repulsive and delightful, buildings, everything caught his attention.

A few people walked around with various kinds of drinks and food. He mostly saw bread, which made sense. It was an easy food to eat while standing around.

A young boy about nine or ten years old walked a few feet behind Alroy. His clothes were worn, dirty, and his hygiene was no better. He was probably a beggar.

Alroy ignored him and focused on his surroundings

and finding the Globe. The lad became the background to the bigger picture.

The boy knocked into him and moved on.

"Hey." Richard shouted. "That boy picked your pocket."

Alroy grabbed the pouch on his belt. It was gone. He hadn't felt anything. The boy must have cut the purse.

Alroy spotted the boy up ahead, turning into a side street. Richard rushed after the boy, and Alroy followed.

"Out of my way. Thief. Thief," Alroy shouted.

The crowd parted, making way for him. He pushed himself to run faster. The boy swerved right then left, putting people between him and Richard.

Breathing hard, Alroy picked up speed. He was more worried about catching Richard than the boy. When his friend was drinking, he was capable of doing any number of stupid things.

Then Alroy remembered that his EB was in the pouch. This is bad, very bad. Leaving future technology in the past is a major issue. He kept Richard and the boy in sight, following them through every turn until he realized they were going in circles. The thief managed to stay ahead of them.

Another two turns, and he realized he was lost, but it didn't matter. Catching the boy and getting the EB back mattered. If he didn't find his way back to the POD and if he lost his EB, he'd be stuck here.

The others would probably leave, expecting him to use his Emergence Button. Then there was the fact that if the boy accidentally pushed the button, he'd be teleported to TTU.

He lost sight of Richard and the boy. Stopping, he

turned three times, sweeping the area for any sign of Richard and the boy. Nothing. He'd turned to try and retrace his path, when he spotted a shadow.

The boy squatted behind a wooden box a few feet away. Alroy slowly moved forward. Relief swept over him. Losing an EB would have been a big problem.

Travelers were supposed to guard the technology. He'd been so enamored with his surroundings and annoyed with Richard he'd let down his guard. Well, he wouldn't do that again.

Richard was nowhere in sight.

A few feet before Alroy reached the box, the boy popped up and bolted away. He managed to keep out front. They raced until Alroy's lungs were on fire. Breathing in the toxic air wasn't helping.

The boy turned into an alley. Alroy pushed himself to run faster. The alley was empty except for the boy scrambling up a wooden fence.

Rushing forward, Alroy leaped into the air, caught the thief by an ankle, and pulled him down. They both crashed into the dirt. He was sure his face landed in excrement. He tried not to think about it.

The boy was up, but Alroy was faster and yanked him by his tunic, pulling him back.

"My purse."

"What purse?"

Alroy squeezed this boy's wrist until his hand opened, exposing the bag in his grubby hand. Holding onto the boy, he took the bag. The boy kicked him in his shin, but Alroy expected the kick and the pain.

Gripping the boy with one hand, he opened the purse, glanced in and saw the EB.

"Why'd you take this?" Alroy demanded.

"To sell. I got a ma and sister to feed."

The boy was as skinny as a small twig. His cheeks sunk in and his skin sallow.

"I'll give you a coin, if you lead me back to my friends. Get yourself some food."

"You ain't serious."

"I'm not from around here. I don't know the way."

The boy grinned. "You're a right crazy fellow, walkin' around with your purse danglin'. I'm surprised you got as far as you did without someone conking you on the head."

Lavinia had warned him. He should have listened.

"How much coin? Let me see it."

Alroy had no idea what the coins were worth. The boy was so thin and sickly, he figured it wouldn't hurt if he gave him too much. He pulled out three coins and placed them in the palm of his hand. The boy's eyes grew wide, and he glanced up at Alroy with a look of awe.

"I'd give ye a tour of London for that."

Alroy relaxed his grip on the boy. Lightning fast, the little pickpocket thief kicked him in the shins, grabbed the coins, and took off running. He watched the boy, shrugged, and walked out of the alley.

In the future, he'd know better than to gape like a fool or to display his bag. He chuckled. Apparently he wasn't intelligent enough to listen to his own advice. Lavinia would definitely rub it in.

He didn't blame the boy. Alroy was street smart in his time, but here he was an easy mark.

The challenge now was to find the others. He'd missed his chance to see Julius Caesar. He ignored the heavy feeling in his chest and told himself he might have another opportunity to visit Shakespeare's London. He hoped the girls saw the play and that somehow Richard had found the POD.

He wandered around, asking for directions to the Globe, getting lost again. Finally, he stepped into an alley.

"Bella," he said.

"I'm here."

She didn't appear in her holograph form, which was best considering that someone seeing her would cause just as much trouble as someone stealing his EB and using it.

"I lost Richard."

"He's with the others. They went into the play."

Alroy sighed. "Good. Did you know Richard is a drinker?"

"No. Should I make a note of that?"

He shook his head until he realized she couldn't see him.

"No. I'll talk to him. Maybe I can talk him into getting help. Can you lead me back to the POD."

"I sent a map. Check your personal computer."

The map helped. He'd been closer than he thought. His worry now was passing the exam. When he located the POD, he walked to the Globe, but they wouldn't let him inside.

It was getting late, there were fewer people on the muddy streets. His pant legs were covered with mud, mostly from running through the streets. Returning to the POD, he pulled up a recording of *Julius Caesar* that was performed last year in the modern Globe Theatre. Not quite the same, but it was the best he could do. He's finished watching the play, when he heard Lavinia's voice outside the POD.

All three walked into the POD praising the theater, the actors, and the play. He smiled, trying not to be jealous or depressed that he may have failed the exam.

That night Lavinia came to his room and offered to help him write up what they saw and experienced. It would be a lie to say he wasn't tempted. He was very tempted, but in the end he had the courage to take responsibility for his actions.

At the door, Lavinia turned back. "You know Teresa has a crush on you."

He grimaced. "I noticed. We need to put a stop to it."

"We?"

"Yes, we. I suspect you've encouraged her. Don't forget I'm an adventurer. Not looking for a relationship."

She studied him for an uncomfortable moment. "I have encouraged her. I'm not sure if she is that serious. But I'm curious . . . are you planning to take up with women of dubious background?"

"Maybe. Some people might think I'm of dubious background."

"And your mother?"

"My mother will never know."

"Well, there's that."

The next afternoon, Alroy was summoned to Professor Skyles' office. Like his classroom, his office had several dozen paintings, photographs, and sketches on the wall. He sat behind his wide mahogany desk and looked up when Alroy entered. He pointed to the leather chair that faced his desk.

Alroy sat and waited. His lunch churned in his stomach and threatened to come up. He took a deep breath and prepared himself for the worst. Yesterday, he'd longed for the freedom of going back to 1890 and living a normal life. Today, he realized that was the last thing he wanted.

"Well, Alroy, it seems you've had another adventure. You have a knack for those."

"Yes, sir."

"Your PEB was stolen and you had a choice. Get it back or leave it in the past. For the record, you made the correct choice. I'm sorry you missed the play. Your companions' reports suggested the play was excellent."

Since Skyles didn't immediately fail him, he had a little hope that perhaps he hadn't completely failed. At least, he hoped.

"There are two other students who also had issues and didn't complete the assignment. You can take a C- for this exam, or you can accompany them back and see another play, *Midsummer Night's Dream*. The choice is yours."

"*Midsummer Night's Dream*, of course."

Alroy's entire body relaxed. He'd never thought of Skyles as generous or helpful. The surprise was pleasant.

"Lavinia volunteered to be the lead on this trip." The professor grinned. "I suspect she'd like to see another play. She was so impressed I'm hoping she doesn't run away to become an actress."

After a few more pleasantries, Alroy rose to leave. "One question, sir. Was this plan Lavinia's idea?"

"No. It was mine. When I went through the training, I also got my pocket picked in London. You might say that I sympathize with your predicament."

Alroy left smiling and well aware that things could have been far worse. He did have a propensity for getting into trouble.

Particularly when he didn't listen to his peers. Especially Lavinia. She wasn't a woman to be ignored. In his mind she could do and be anything she wanted.

He was actually whistling when he walked into the dining room to sweet-talk the cook into giving him a piece of pie.

Author of *League of the Daring*
CORA FOERSTNER
Guardian:
Friend or Foe?
Some helpers make things worse!

Guardian: Friend or Foe?

Lavinia sat on the balcony outside her dorm room. She pulled the comb through her curly black hair. It was damp from her shower. The conditioner she used had a coconut smell and made her hair shine.

She lifted her face toward the sunshine and closed her eyes. Sometimes she missed the warmth of sunny days in Los Angeles. She considered that longing nostalgia for home and reminded herself that her time at the Time Travel University was coming to an end.

After she'd combed her curly hair straight, she rolled it with extra large curlers. When she'd finished, her head looked as if she'd wrapped her hair in toilet paper rolls. Although the sun wasn't as warm as her California sun, it would be dry by the time she needed to meet her friends for their time travel assignment.

Next week they were graduating, and still no one knew where they would go afterwards. That worried her. Not so much because the destination was unknown, but because she didn't want to continue living here.

She and Alroy talked it over last night. They both wanted to be in a real city somewhere in the twenty-first century, and preferably somewhere sunny.

The university wasn't a bad place, but they'd been cooped up here for five years with the same people. Sure, new students came in and a few left, but she missed the real world.

Unlike the others, she and Alroy had been on Guardian Hubs, which could be made to look like anything. This one looked like a university, but she and Alroy knew it wasn't real. After five years, some of her friends believed them.

She knew that if there were windows to the outside, the students would see they hung somewhere in space. The first time she saw space, she panicked inside but showed a calm face to her friends, pretending she wasn't terrified.

If the other students considered their surroundings, there were plenty of clues, like seventy-degree weather year round, perfect crops in their garden, no wildlife or insects, no rain or snow or freezing nights. Even the deserts in California got cold at night.

Students used portals to go home for holidays. They had no need to leave the university. Everything they needed was here.

Going home should have been the clue everyone needed to understand.

She noticed how different the outside world was. She missed people, news, new clothing styles, a variety of food, and all the things living in society offered. On their visits home, she also realized she no longer belonged in the 1890s. Now 1896 because they'd left in 1891. She knew too much to be content there.

At home, her friends seemed quaint and naive. It wasn't fair to think that way, but she did. She'd once believed that she loved Pedro and always would. When she returned home the first time, the old spark was gone.

She suspected it was gone for him too. He was always kind, but never romantic.

A pounding at her door interrupted her thoughts. For a few moments, she ignored it, hoping whoever it was would go away. But they didn't.

She walked into her room, which was a replica of her room in Los Angeles down to the canopy bed with the gauze fabric painted with red roses. Bella, her AI friend, helped her and got every detail right. In five years, Lavinia never changed a thing. In a world where everything was strange, this room comforted her.

When she opened the door, Teresa had her hand raised as if to knock again.

"Finally."

Teresa's long dark brown hair was pulled back in a braid that hung down her back in a thick coil. She was from 1905 Spain. Since coming here she always dressed in jeans and t-shirts. Lavinia admitted they gave more freedom than the volumes of material in the dresses they wore at home.

Teresa's brown eyes sparkled with excitement or some less positive emotion. She was shorter and more curvy than Lavinia, which the boys found attractive. These last few months Teresa had only had eyes for Alroy, and

Lavinia guessed he would ignore her until she gave up. He wasn't much for personal confrontation.

"What's so urgent?"

"There's a Guardian here. He's asking for you. He wanted to come up here, but Mr. Skyles insisted I come for you." Teresa giggled. "The teachers are acting like giddy teenagers."

Lavinia patted her hair. It was still damp. "He'll have to wait until my hair is dry."

"Use the hair dryer."

"No. I don't like it."

Teresa grabbed her by the arm and dragged her toward the bathroom. "You can't keep a Guardian waiting. I'm missing out on what's happening. So hurry."

Lavinia sighed and allowed Teresa to dry her hair. The heat of the coils gave off a damp sort of burnt smell as if her hair was about to catch fire. She told herself that wasn't the case. The hot air blowing across her face and on her neck felt good.

"Is this man tall with blondish brown hair? Does he wear all black? Did he tell you what your name means?"

Teresa turned off the blow dryer. "Yes, exactly. He said, 'Teresa, late summer or to harvest.' I never knew my name was so lame."

"He's Raymond, protector of men and women." Lavinia began pulling the curlers out of her hair.

"You know a real Guardian."

She continued staring at herself in the mirror. Living in this environment her bronze skin had gotten lighter. She didn't know if that was good or bad. Probably neither. No one really cared. She ran her brush through her hair.

"I'm sure Alroy has told everyone about Raymond."

"Yes, but we all thought he was lying."

"Alroy has his faults, but blatant lying isn't among them."

She knew that wasn't true. He'd lied to the League of the Daring when he was drinking. But that was long ago. For all practical purposes, he was truthful. Hiding his own personal secret may not count.

"Trust me," she said to Teresa, "don't get excited about Raymond. If he's here, that means there's some kind of trouble on the horizon. I'd be better off hiding."

"You can't mean that."

"I do. Pray he doesn't notice you."

"He already has."

"Well, that can't be undone. Let us go to whatever doom awaits us."

"You exaggerate."

Lavinia sighed. She hoped she was wrong, but she was certain Raymond's presence meant he wanted her and, no doubt, Alroy to do something for him.

He meant well, so she couldn't fault him for wanting to help them, but he always threw them into a dangerous situation. Come to think of it, time travel inevitably turned dangerous.

They met Alroy in the first floor hallway hurrying toward the dining room.

"Bella said Raymond wants us."

She nodded. They found Raymond in the dining room surrounded by teachers and students pelting him with questions and vying to get closer to him. The Guardian frowned. His bushy brows came together as he listened to Professor Skyles.

When he spotted Lavinia and Alroy, he straightened and smiled.

"Wow, he recognizes you," Teresa whispered.

Raymond pushed his way through the crowd, moving toward them as Professor Skyles turned to follow him.

As Raymond walked away, he waved his hand and a glass-like dome descended on everyone. Almost immediately, students began beating on the glass and shouting as they stared at him.

Alroy pointed to the students and teachers. "They are going to be angry."

"Nonsense. They are noisy, and we need to talk."

"Let them out, and we can go somewhere quiet," Lavinia said.

Raymond waved his hand again and lifted the dome. Another wave of his hand and the tables were filled with a feast.

"We are going somewhere quiet to talk," Raymond called out. "Enjoy the feast."

Professor Skyles ignored him and followed them. "We can go to my office," he said as he hurried to catch up to them.

Raymond stopped abruptly and glared down at the professor, who squirmed slightly under his gaze.

"Delbert, why are you following us?"

Lavinia watched as Skyles stood his ground and faced Raymond, who could become very intimidating.

"Two reasons, these students are under my care, and I

must make sure they are safe. Secondly, this is finals week and they have to finish their training."

"Um, I am a Guardian who watches over this dimension. Do you really expect me to harm them?" Raymond's eyebrows rose as he waited for an answer.

Lavinia almost giggled. Teresa, not side tracked by the feast, poked Lavinia and frowned.

Raymond was not human, and he often imitated people so that he looked more human. She was certain his raised eyebrows were an imitation of Wyatt, Alroy's brother.

"Certainly not. I never meant to imply such a thing."

"Well, the implication was clear. And what is this silly business about a final?"

"All students must complete five time travel tests to be qualified to become a time traveler."

Raymond glanced at Lavinia and then Alroy as if asking if this were true. Alroy nodded.

"Nonsense, these two have traveled more than you have. They have rescued their friends from kidnappers, solved murders, and helped Grace and me several times."

This time Professor Skyles' eyebrows rose. "They didn't put that on their applications."

"I suspect they are modest. Now, lead the way to your office."

The professor's shoulders sagged as he walked down the long, too bright hallway. They climbed a flight of stairs to Skyles' office, which was a corner office with windows. Everyone in this century seemed to think of that as a status symbol.

Lavinia thought the idea silly, but since they didn't

really get to mingle with the people of this century, she faulted the faculty and not herself for not understanding the implications.

When they entered the room, Raymond took a deep breath, and spoke. "Everything I say cannot be repeated. Is that understood? None of you can repeat this to anyone."

Lavinia, Alroy, and Teresa immediately agreed. Raymond stared at Skyles.

"Oh, surely you don't mean me."

Raymond waved his hand, and a small dome with a chair inside surrounded the professor.

"You are not winning friends doing that," Lavinia said.

"I'm not trying to win friends. The man is tedious."

Skyles cupped his hands around his mouth and shouted. Or at least, Lavinia assumed he shouted. She couldn't hear him.

"For heaven's sakes." Raymond waved his hand and the dome vanished.

"I agree. I agree," the professor repeated.

Raymond squinted at him and nodded. He rubbed his hands together, which was a bad sign that he was about to tell them something he thought was exciting. Unfortunately, his exciting plans usually turned out to be something crazy.

"I would like for you to come with me. Including you, Teresa. Bella says you are quite accomplished."

"How would Bella know that?" Skyles asked.

"Bella monitors everything at TTU. Now—"

"Well, we will have to put a stop to that." Skyles took a small notebook out of his pants' pocket and wrote a note.

"Delbert, you do understand who I am, don't you?"

"Yes, of course, you're a Guardian."

"I am the Guardian who oversees all human dimensions and societies."

"Oh." Skyles grinned. "You're important. I understand that, but I run TTU, and I—"

Raymond snapped his fingers and Skyles vanished.

"Oh, my," Teresa said and sank into the closest chair. "Did you kill him?"

Lavinia pressed her lips together to keep from laughing, while Alroy glanced from Teresa to Raymond.

"Certainly not," Raymond finally said. "I don't kill people."

"Where is he?" Alroy asked.

"Oh, he's perfectly safe." Raymond pointed to a poster of the Eiffel Tower. "He's there. I'll return him when we're finished. He keeps interrupting."

Lavinia studied the poster. Under the photograph was the date 1943. She didn't know the significance of the date, but she did know that the Nazis occupied France in 1943.

"Please tell me you didn't send him into the past." Lavinia crossed her arms and stared at him.

Teresa stared at Raymond with wide eyes. Her face looked about four shades lighter than normal. Lavinia's mother would have said she looked pallid. Lavinia thought her friend might faint.

"Of course, I sent him to the past. That large picture had a date. I assumed he favored that date. He does study your history, right? He must be pleased."

"Oh, no," Teresa whispered. "Nazis."

She bent forward and placed her hands over her face

whispering something. Lavinia assumed she was praying for Profess Skyles, but maybe she was praying for herself. Alroy stared at Raymond as if he were in shock.

"Nazis," Raymond repeated. "Ah, Delbert must be a World War II expert. He'll be fine."

Teresa jumped up. "He is not fine! He's in danger. You must bring him back at once. At once!"

"Is this true?" Raymond looked at Alroy first and then at Lavinia.

"Yes. It is true. You may have sent the poor man to his doom." For emphasis, Lavinia crossed her arms and frowned.

"That's a bit melodramatic," Raymond said.

Bella appeared by Raymond's side. "No, it is not. German soldiers climbed the tower, where you placed him, and arrested him."

Their personal computers pinged. Lavinia glanced at the photo Bella sent them. There on the front page of a French newspaper were several pictures of Professor Skyles.

The first one showed him two thirds of the way up the tower hanging on for his life. The painful look of fear on his face shocked Lavinia. Her heart did a jump, skip sort of beat. The next photo was him being hauled away by two men in uniform. Secret service? Gestapo?

"Bella," Alroy said. "Translate the headline."

Bella's hologram appeared. "The SS captured the Leader of the French Resistance."

"Well, um." Raymond frowned. "I guess we'll have to go find him. He should have stayed put."

Lavinia didn't speak and gave Teresa a slight shake of

the head. Talking would delay them. They needed to hurry.

An hour later, with blond wigs, 1940s clothing, and a feeling of terror, Lavinia entered the POD, their Poly-Occupant Device, where Raymond, Teresa, and Alroy were waiting for her. A POD held six people and was equipped with supplies to sustain six people for a week.

Each POD also had Guardian stealth technology that allowed them to park the vehicle and not be noticed. Usually they tucked the POD in a corner somewhere where people wouldn't be likely to trip over it.

Because of her dark skin, Lavinia would easily be noticed among the French and Germans. She had to stay in the POD and monitor the situation. She wasn't happy, but she realized she'd stand out and be noticed immediately. Someone had to stay behind, it might as well be her.

"Everyone have their translators?" Alroy asked. "We can move back and forth between French and German depending on who we need to talk to."

"Remember, I cannot interfere with human interactions," Raymond said. "So this rescue has to be done by Alroy and Teresa. Understood?"

Of course, Lavinia knew that was nonsense. He would interfere. She'd seen him do just that. He'd already interfered.

Bella found two locations where she thought the SS might have taken Professor Skyles. Both were near the Eiffel Tower.

At Raymond's direction and with Bella's coordinates, Lavinia piloted the POD. They parked near the middle of the tower off to the south, near a building with a small alleyway that dead ended. Sunset was at nine fifty-five.

They arrived at nine and used the camera to scan the alley and the area around the Eiffel Tower. Relief settled in Lavinia as her shoulders relaxed.

The alley was clear, there were people in the streets, but the crowds were obviously thinning. She stiffened when she spotted German military and French National Police, collaborators with the Nazis. They seemed to be intermingled with the people. Lavinia watched for a while and realized that most people averted their eyes or casually turned away.

She wished she had eaten because her stomach seemed to be an acid factory. This was far more dangerous than anything they'd done before. She wished that Raymond would just go in and rescue the professor. She knew he could do it. Plus she knew he wouldn't.

The Guardians watched humans as if they were nothing but science projects. They wanted to see what humans would do, not direct their course, which was why only a few Guardians took an interest in human affairs. Most of them had decided that humans were too violent and not likely to evolve.

Of course, Lavinia disagreed. Human society might evolve slowly, but two steps forward and one step back was still progress. She wasn't about to dismiss humans as hopeless.

"Look." Teresa said, pointing to her camera.

High up on the Eiffel Tower, the Swastika of the Nazi flag stood out. Bile burned Lavinia's throat.

Lavinia swiveled in her chair. "Raymond, this is too dangerous."

"Nonsense. Travelers are often put into dangerous situations."

He tossed each of them a small cube attached to what looked like a keychain with a sturdy safety pen attached to the chain.

"Attach this in a convenient place you can reach in an instant. Pressing the button will bring you back to the POD."

He tossed one to Lavinia.

"You too. For safety."

She glanced at the cube as if it were a snake. Raymond knew something she didn't. That worried her.

Twenty minutes later as dusk settled over the city and fewer people were on the streets, Raymond, Alroy, and Teresa slipped out of the POD.

Lavinia used the window and computer screens to watch them as they made their way down the alley and into the street. A few seconds later, the camera lost sight of them.

Her only connection now would be Bella, who could communicate with them more easily than she could. She watched the screens as it grew dark outside, a dangerous time for anyone to be on the street.

Then she paced and glanced at her watch. The minutes passed like hours. She hated being the one left behind. At least if she were with them, she could make decisions and know what was happening. Now all she could do was wait and hope.

Bella's hologram appeared beside her. She jumped and squealed.

"Sorry. Didn't mean to frighten you. They searched the first building. It's abandoned. I'll let you know when they reach the second building."

"Thank you. Keep your hologram here. I'm jumpy."

"Would you like me to talk to you and distract you?"

"No." Lavinia felt as if she shouted. "Sorry. I don't want to be distracted. I want to be alert in case something happens."

Less than five minutes later, Bella's hologram moved. "They have reached the second building. There are people inside. They have stun guns."

"That doesn't make me feel better. The Nazis have real guns that kill people."

"True. They should have taken the sleeping gas."

Lavinia whirled around. "What?'

"Little marble containers that contain a harmless gas that puts people to sleep."

"Wouldn't it put them to sleep as well?"

"Not if you have a mask."

Lavinia wanted to shout at Bella, asking her why she didn't equip them with this sleeping gas, but she didn't. She learned long ago that although Bella seemed real to her, she wasn't. She was more like a living encyclopedia than a person with reasoning skills.

Bella stared at her. "You're right. I should have thought of that."

"Don't tell me you can read my mind? Please, no."

"I can read your face and your body language. You are struggling to contain your anger. I asked myself why, and the only reasonable answer is that I should have thought about sending them out with masks and sleeping gas."

"Well, yes, those were my exact thoughts."

"Alroy is going into the building to see if he can get information," Bella said.

Lavinia took a deep breath and began pacing again. She'd only paced for seconds when a portal opened inside the POD. Teresa stepped through panting as if she'd been running. She bent over and gasped for breath.

Every fiber of Lavinia's being wanted to scream at Teresa and force her to explain. Instead, she glanced at Bella because she knew the little AI girl had direct communications with Raymond.

"What's going on?"

It was Teresa who answered. "They took Alroy. Raymond vanished and told me to wait. I did until two policemen rounded the corner and found me. I pressed the cube."

She sank down into the nearest chair and sighed. Lavinia wasn't in the mood to give her a pep talk. This was actually the kind of test they needed to see who had what it took to make decisions in difficult circumstances.

"Bella, where is the sleeping gas? And the masks?"

Bella's hologram pointed to the cabinet.

"Masks on the fifth shelf and sleeping gas bombs next to them."

Lavinia took the small stepladder and used it to reach the bombs, an incredibly terrible term to use for these gadgets. They turned out to be plastic pods about the size of a golf ball. She grabbed three boxes and five masks.

The masks were definitely Guardian tech. She grabbed

one. A clear plastic-like substance covered the entire face. She put it up to her face, and it immediately shaped itself to her face.

She could breathe and see perfectly. There was oxygen. The mask stayed in place. She didn't bother to question Bella about the technology. She asked about the logistics of using the gas and the mask.

"As you see, the mask will automatically shape to a person's face. Your problem will be getting the mask on them before throwing the sleeping gas. There is a filtration system built into the mask. It turns gas particles into solid and prevents them from getting into the person's body. The air you breathe will be pure. To use the gas, crush the ball in your hand and toss it into the room. It's an invisible gas that will work within ten seconds."

Ten seconds. That was enough time for soldiers to shoot.

Lavinia pushed the thought out of her mind and filled her pockets with sleeping gas and grabbed another box. She tossed Teresa a mask.

"Put that on." She held out the box of sleeping gas bombs. "Fill your pockets with these and take an extra mask. I'll take the other two."

Teresa stood up, shaking her head and holding her hand up as if she were refusing Lavinia's offer.

"No. No. I'm not going back there."

"Bella, change your appearance. Male, SS, high ranking soldier. You're going with us. Make yourself opaque so you look real."

Lavinia grabbed two stun guns with tranquilizer darts. She tossed one to Teresa. She'd used one of these when they rescued Elijah from some rogue time travelers. She stepped off the stepladder and faced Teresa.

"I'm not going out there," Teresa said.

"Do you want to be a time traveler?"

"Yes. You know I do."

"When you travel, things like this happen. Either you act and do the best you can with what you have, or you're not going to make a time traveler. The tests we've been taking are designed for children to play at time travel. Our professor and our friends are in trouble. Are you coming or are you going to huddle in the corner and fret?"

Teresa took a deep breath and stared at Lavinia. She pressed her lips together. As the seconds ticked by, Lavinia tried to imagine doing this by herself with Bella dressed as a Nazi.

"Okay. But I'm terrified."

"Only a fool wouldn't be terrified. Here's the plan. Bella will be with us, and anyone on the streets at night will try to hide from the authorities. Those on the streets are authorities. They'll see us and let us pass. If anyone is outside the building, we throw the sleeping gas. If anyone attacks, we shoot them. The gun has tranquilizers. We won't be harming anyone."

"What about finding Alroy and Professor Skyles?"

"We search. We use the sleeping gas when necessary. When we find them, try to get them a mask. If we can't, we throw the gas. We'll figure it out from there."

If Lavinia thought Teresa looked pale earlier, she looked terrifyingly ghastly now. Teresa swallowed and nodded.

Bella reappeared as a SS soldier. Teresa jumped and yelled. Their favorite AI had disappeared, and a rather terrifying man with blond hair, broad shoulders, and a turned down mouth appeared.

Bella smiled. "From your response, I guess my costume is convincing."

"Hide the dart gun inside you coat." Lavinia demonstrated. "Let's go."

As they stepped out of the alley, Lavinia glanced up at the dark Eiffel Tower. Although it was dark and she couldn't actually see the swastika on the flag, she imagined it.

The streets were empty. Not just empty but dark. No lights showed in windows, no streetlights were lit, and silence wrapped around Lavinia like a boa trying to squeeze the life out of her.

The parked cars looked like mere shadows until they got closer. Two men stepped out of an alley, saw them, and ran.

Bella led them forward. They took so many turns that Lavinia lost count of the streets and which turns they made. She was hopelessly lost. If their cubes failed and if their PEBs failed, which they never had, they would be caught by Nazis.

Pushing the thought out of her mind, she marched forward. A patrol of three men marched toward them, shining their flashlights down alleys and checking doors. As they approached them, one of the men shouted stop, which she and Teresa did. Bella continued forward.

As she approached the men, they stiffened and saluted.

They couldn't hear the exchange, but the men hurried away. Bella waved them forward.

"I frightened them with a very deep voice." She giggled.

"This isn't a game," Lavinia said.

"Maybe it is. This way." She turned the corner onto a very narrow street.

The next block they turned right. Lavinia realized her eyes had adjusted to the darkness, making it easier to move faster. Bella stopped in front of an old dingy building, the plaster on the walls pealed away. Blackout curtains in the window helped shroud the door in shadows.

Lavinia stepped up to the door and reached into her pocket to take out two balls of sleeping gas. She pounded on the door.

Once. Twice. Three times. No one answered.

She shouted. "Open up now."

The handle turned and Lavinia stepped sideways letting Bella stand in front of the door. The man who opened the door stared, stiffened, and saluted.

"Sorry, sir. I had no idea. Come in."

"Step aside," Bella said, her voice deep and threatening.

When the man stepped back, Lavinia squeezed the balls of gas and thew them inside. She waited four beats before stepping inside. Three men coughed, clutched their throats, and slipped to the floor. Lavinia glanced at Teresa, who stared at the men but followed her inside.

"I scanned the building. Alroy and Professor Skyles are in separate rooms beyond that door."

Lavinia glanced back, expecting to have to encourage

Teresa to follow them. She knelt down beside one of the fallen men searching his pocket. She held up two sets of keys.

Lavinia tried the door. It was locked. No surprise there. Teresa tried several keys until she found the right one.

"Step back," Lavinia said. "I'm going to open the door. Bella you go in first. Say 'clear' if the hall is empty. 'Gas' if there are people."

"I think you've been watching too many cop shows," Teresa said.

Two seconds later, Bella shouted, "Gas."

Two balls of sleeping gas in hand, Lavinia entered and tossed the gas into the center of the four men gathered around Bella. Seconds later, the men grabbed their throats.

In rapid succession, the men fainted. Lavinia pointed to the first locked door and waited with a ball ready as Teresa opened the door.

Alroy sat naked except for his boxer shorts on a metal chair in the middle of the room. He grinned when he saw them. He didn't look as if he'd been beaten or abused.

"Took you long enough. Don't look so puzzled, Lavinia. I think this is some kind of torture or fear tactic. The professor is across the hall. For some reason, I think Raymond might be down the hall. I heard him talking to the men. I'd like to find my clothes and my tech."

Lavinia tossed him a mask. "Put that on before the gass seeps into this room."

"What gas?" he asked as he slipped the mask onto his face.

They found the professor in the room across the hall. He lay on the floor, naked, bloody, and unconscious. Bella hovered over him. Apparently, Bella didn't need the door opened to get to him. She glanced up.

"He has a broken arm, no internal damage, and will recover. Raymond is next door, waiting to be rescued."

"That's silly," Lavinia said. "He can get out by himself." She was far more worried about the professor than she was about rescuing someone who didn't need rescuing.

"I'll get him, " Teresa said.

Moments later she and Raymond returned. A few seconds later, Alroy returned dressed and held out his tech for them to see.

"Oddly, they didn't take any interest in these."

Bella opened a portal. Raymond took the professor directly to the university.

Alroy, Lavinia, and a reluctant Teresa searched all the rooms making sure that nothing from their visit remained. They found a couple forms with the professor and Alroy's names and took all the papers that referenced the professor or Alroy.

They used Raymond's device to return to the POD. Within an hour they were back at the school, confronted by the other teachers and making a statement about their experience.

That night Teresa and Alroy sneaked into Lavinia's room. They sat on the floor in front of her fireplace drinking hot chocolate and discussing their adventure.

"The doctor said the professor will be fine. Mrs. Herbert is angry and wants us expelled," Teresa said.

"That's not going to happen," Alroy said. "Raymond

told me that was our final exam. He threatened to take all the teachers and students on an outing."

Teresa leaned forward and stared at the fire. "I thought you were being dramatic when you told me about Raymond. He's quite frightening."

Lavinia only nodded. You had to experience Raymond to understand. Now Teresa understood.

"My guess is he'll put the other students to the test. Some will decide they like being support." Alroy shrugged.

"Raymond said something about Bella helping to train the students," Teresa said. "Is that who trained the League of the Daring?"

Lavinia nodded and grinned. They lifted the hot chocolate mugs and toasted to their success.

Author of *League of the Daring*

CORA FOERSTNER

Hidden Things

What lurks below?

Hidden Things

Alroy stood at his dorm room window looking down at the quad. The Time Travel University buildings formed a horseshoe shape. He studied the buildings, considering the five floors in each building.

He and the students he started with five years ago were ready to graduate. Now he was curious why a few students needed an enormously large campus.

The sugary sweet smell of cinnamon rolls filled the hallway and seeped into his room. Ronald loved baking. When he went home he brought back baking supplies. Students weren't supposed to cook in their rooms. He did. No one told anyone he broke the rules because his baked goods were too good.

But right now, what caught Alroy's attention was the university campus. The small student body and the handful of teachers basically lived and worked on two floors of the massive compound. The white outside walls and the large windows that let in light looked pristine.

The carefully landscaped exteriors were expansive enough for a large university and thousands of students.

This place was built for more than teaching thirty students how to time travel. Just as Lavinia suggested, something else was going on here.

Glancing at his watch, he realized he'd been standing here thinking for over an hour. He chided himself for allowing Lavinia's questions about where they went after graduation to get to him. Her theory was that the teachers, the older time travelers, and the Guardians planned on keeping them here. Not as prisoners, but that's what they'd be if Lavinia was right.

Originally, he'd dismissed the idea, but as he looked at the buildings, he realized there were areas of the school they'd never visited or seen.

Yesterday, Teresa told him she found a door that led to a basement. She followed the stairs down three levels before getting spooked and coming back up. He was meeting her in a few minutes to go down with her and explore.

The information didn't frighten him, but it did disturb him. He felt as if all Lavinia's fears about being stuck here forever couldn't be dismissed. He didn't want to spend his life inside a small community. He wanted to explore the world. That was his primary reason for becoming a time traveler. He wanted to live in the world and experience life.

He'd composed a message and sent it to Raymond. He explained Lavinia's fears and his apprehensions. He didn't think anyone came here expecting to be isolated from society. Dystopian novels came to mind.

If anyone knew and could change things, it was a Guardian. But would he?

The League of the Daring realized years ago that Guardians weren't human. Lately, Lavinia had developed another theory. Guardians were actually people. People who had advanced mentally, surpassing them in every way. All time travel abilities and technology came from the Guardians.

Alroy found it easier to believe that Raymond and the others were advanced beings than that they were mentally advanced people.

From the history he'd learned about them, they were scientists only interested in studying humans, human societies, and their evolution. Most Guardians had given up on the human experiment and stopped watching and studying them. They saw human history as a trajectory toward violence and extinction.

Sometimes he thought they were right. Other times, he believed people could become better.

He sighed and stared at the quad. A concrete sidewalk wide enough for three or four students to walk side by side ran along the outside and was empty. The two-foot-tall red brick fence surrounded the quad except for the three openings that faced each of the buildings.

The south side of the quad looked like a park with grass, evergreen trees, and strategically placed benches. Alroy's favorite spot was the large koi pond in the center of the park area. The water and the fish left him feeling tranquil. When he needed quiet and peace, he went there. He tried to imagine a life where the only people he knew were the selected few time travelers and support staff. The thought made him shudder.

He spotted Lavinia on the other side of the quad where tables with umbrellas dotted the brick patio. She sat at a table staring off into space as if lost in thought. If she had one defect, it was thinking too much.

He took out his personal computer and sent her a message.

Are you coming with us to the basement?

A few seconds ticked by before he saw her reach for her handheld computer.

Yes. Have you heard from Raymond?

No.

You believe me now?

Maybe. I have questions. I'm heading down now. Meet me outside the cafeteria.

He watched as she gathered her belongings. Then he crossed his room, zigzagging around the furniture as he made his way to the door.

Most of the other students had replicated their bedrooms at home. He hadn't. This room was a compilation of furniture and trinkets he'd collected from history, or had duplicated from images and his historical research. His belongings could fill a small apartment.

A small Victorian mahogany table sat by his door. He ran his hand over the rich smooth wood of the varnished top as he passed.

This piece he'd duplicated from his home. One exactly like it sat in the entryway in his mother's house in Los Angeles in 1896. On both tables a candlestick telephone sat in the center. Hers worked. His didn't. This was his nod to his other life and his family.

Slipping out into the empty hallway, he hurried to the end of the hall and took the stairs down to the next floor. Like everything in this building, the walls were white and the floor tiles were black and white. The only color and interest came from the students, who were hungry for variety, textures, and color.

Lavinia stood outside the cafeteria waiting for him. Her black hair, pulled back and twisted up into a bun, framed her face, showing off her classic beauty.

His friend Toby once said she looked like a bronze statue of a goddess. Alroy agreed. She was tall, slender, and full of righteous wrath when it suited her.

Teresa, her opposite, stood next to her leaning against the white wall saying something to Lavinia, who smiled. Her wavy, long brown hair hung past her shoulders. While Lavinia frightened people, Teresa's softness disguised a woman who championed the underdog.

Theo jogged down the hall toward the girls. He always wore Hawaiian shirts with big flowers, his blond hair was pulled back in a ponytail, and a wide smile rarely left his face. Slowing, he approached Alroy and handed him one of the backpacks he carried over his shoulder.

"Flashlights and some things I thought might come in handy." Theo's voice sounded lazy and soft, another person disguising his true nature.

His presence calmed people. He claimed surfing gave people a sense of calm. Alroy wouldn't be surprised if that were true.

Lavinia and Teresa detached themselves from the wall, and Teresa led them down the hallway to the girl's bathroom.

"In there?" Theo asked. "Dude, you need to check and make sure it's empty. I get into enough trouble without getting busted for sneaking into the girl's room."

Lavinia chuckled and followed Teresa into the bathroom. "All clear," she called out.

Teresa stood at the back of the bathroom holding a closet door open.

"Let me guess," Alroy said. "A secret door at the back of the closet?"

Teresa nodded and pushed on the opening between two shelves that held cleaning supplies and linens. A wide door opened and a bright light came on, triggered by motion.

Yes, Alroy had learned a few things since coming forward in time.

Teresa waved them through. Alroy glanced back after he had entered. Teresa stepped inside and pushed a button on the wall that closed the door. Good to know, in case they had to hurry out of here.

The staircase was wide, sturdy, and made of something that looked like marble. People could pass each other going up and down the stairs. This was built for a lot of traffic.

Why was this hidden in a closet? Something was definitely up with all this secrecy. As they descended the steps more lights came on, illuminating a long staircase.

Below, the room seemed expansive, like an empty warehouse that went on and on and waited to be filled.

Behind Alroy Teresa spoke. "There's nothing here. It's an empty room. At the bottom turn left and left for the next staircase."

Lavinia was in the lead, and she followed the instructions. The next level was also empty.

Teresa wanted to show them the third level, which was fine with Alroy. On the way up, he was going to insist on exploring the other two levels. Plus, he was going to call Bella to join them.

On the third level down they waited for Teresa, who moved to the wall next to the staircase and switched several switches. Overhead lights flicked on all over the empty level. At equal distances, Alroy guessed about twenty feet, maybe a little more, smooth floor to ceiling pillars were spaced out.

Teresa pointed directly in front of them. Alroy squinted. In the distance green lights pulsed around what looked like extra wide doors. Their heights and widths were large enough to move pieces of equipment through.

"I didn't stop to count them, but there are lot of doors spaced out around the room," Teresa said. "They freaked me out, and I ran out of here. When you get closer, you'll feel something odd. Come."

She hurried forward with the rest of them rushing to keep up with her. The room was a replica of the school, white walls with black and white flooring.

As they got closer to the door, Alroy felt a vibrating, not sound, but a slight shaking on his skin. It reminded him of the first time he went into a portal.

"You feel it?" Teresa asked.

"Yeah," Theo said.

"Yes. It's like a gentle shake, like the strumming of a portal," Lavinia added.

Alroy simply nodded and hurried forward. It was cold down here. Not the perfect seventy degrees of the school and the campus. The air smelled stale, like someplace where the air didn't circulate.

When he reached the door, he placed his hand on it. The vibrations were coming from the door. He couldn't find a door handle to open it.

"There isn't a handle. I checked," Teresa said. "What do you think?"

"Bella," Alroy shouted. "Bella."

The AI's hologram appeared beside Alroy. The image turned slowly, glancing around.

"I'm scanning. Where are we?"

"I called you to ask you that. What is this place?"

"One moment."

The hologram image slowly turned in a circle, then rapidly moved across the expansive room. They all waited, watching Bella's image move back and forth. She seemed to be studying the pillars, walls, and even the floor. Finally, she vanished and reappeared next to Lavinia.

"This is a Super Hub," Bella said.

"What does that mean?" Teresa asked.

"It means that your school is built on top of a Super Hub only used by Guardians. No human should have access to this."

"Who built the school?" Alroy had a bad feeling about this. He'd already met rogue time travelers who wanted to take control of all the dimensions the Guardians created.

Bella was quiet for a moment. They all waited, knowing she was looking something up and probably contacting Raymond.

"Unknown. Grace found this space when she was looking for a location for the school. I've reviewed all her notes and paperwork. I don't think she knows what this place is."

Bella stepped closer to them until she stood in the center, and they were grouped around her.

"This place doesn't exist in any of the records."

"Does this have anything to do with Dolores and her gang?" Lavinia asked.

Dolores was a rogue time traveler, who was willing to kill to get what she wanted. Alroy knew her from the League of the Daring's run-ins with her and her crew. The Guardians locked them away. Alroy didn't know for sure, but he wondered if their new home was some sort of Guardian prison.

"Maybe," Bella said, answering Lavinia.

"The entrance to these levels is hidden in a closet," Teresa said. "Does that mean anything?"

"Maybe."

"Bella, you aren't being helpful," Alroy said. "Tell us about his place."

The hologram image nodded and pointed to the doors behind them. "Those doors are portals to each dimension. As you know, travel between dimensions has been suspended. So they shouldn't be here."

"The other doors?" Lavinia's voice sounded deep and suspicious.

"This is a portal to the future." She turned to Alroy.

"Remember when you sent Pedro, Zella, and Lavinia to the future?"

Alroy nodded. Of course he remembered, and he prayed she wouldn't say more. He had been secretly drinking and put the wrong coordinates into their POD and sent them centuries into the future. It wasn't one of his finest moments.

Lavinia frowned. "What of it?"

"That portal goes to Orange Hope. The other portals lead to other important points in time. From the beginning until the end."

Teresa stared at the portal leading to Orange Hope. "That's the end of time?"

"Of course not," Bella said. "Time will continue on, but that's as far as this dimension has tracked time. In that future they are trying to rebuild civilization."

"Open it." Lavinia said. "I want to go through and see for myself."

"Wait a second," Teresa said. "That's not a good idea."

"I've been there. I know what it's like. I want to see for myself." Lavinia turned to Bella. "I'm right aren't I? The school is more than it appears to be."

"Yes."

"You can create a window, right?"

Bella nodded.

"Do it." Lavinia demanded.

Bella glanced at Alroy, who nodded.

"Show them where we are."

Bella moved closer to the door in front of them. She pointed her hand at the wall above the door and waved back and forth. A long window appeared. Beyond the window was dark space with distant stars glowing.

It looked like pictures a space station would send back to earth or pictures from a powerful telescope. Darkness, swirling masses of color, and lights. The school hung somewhere in space.

Teresa gasped and stared open mouthed. Theo stepped closer. His face paled, and he pointed as he turned toward Bella.

"Space trash could hit us," Theo said.

"No, there is a protective layer preventing any harm."

Theo glanced at Lavinia. "Sorry for teasing you about . . . a school in space." He pointed to the window. "Dudes, my heart is beating so fast, I might have a heart attack."

"Theo, you are perfectly fine. Your heart is in excellent condition for someone your age." Bella's voice was trying to sound reassuring, but she sounded more like a robot.

"Thank you, Bella. Having a heart attack is . . . I guess you'd call it slang." Theo grinned and winked at Bella.

While Theo joked with Bella, Teresa had been staring out the window. Alroy noticed her face grow pale. When she swayed, Alroy grabbed her.

"You'll get used to it," he whispered.

"Open the portal," Lavinia repeated.

"Raymond should—"

"No. We'll talk to him after, I want you to show them. Even Alroy needs to see. Then we'll tell Raymond about this."

Bella's hologram became more opaque. "I'm going with you."

The door rolled back until the doorway shimmered. Lavinia didn't hesitate, she stepped through. The vibrating sensation surged through her body. It was disconcerting the first time. Now it was familiar. She and the League had traveled many times through portals like this one.

Theo followed her, and Alroy moved forward. He stopped in the doorway and glanced at Teresa, who shook her head. Alroy held his hand out.

"Come on. You don't want to be all alone in the giant room."

"He's right," Bella said.

"I don't want to see the end of the world."

Lavinia stepped back in the room. "Come with us. You need to see what we will become."

Teresa hesitated and finally nodded. She followed Lavinia through the portal.

"Just relax. That vibration is normal. You get used to it," Lavinia whispered.

Alroy stepped through last. He didn't blame Teresa for not wanting to see. He wasn't anxious to see where he sent his friends.

They'd studied history, science, anthropology, zoology, and so much more. Their professors said they were working to make the future better. He wasn't sure if this was what had to happen in the future or if it was one possibility, but he needed to know.

They stood in an overgrown landscape. In the distance, she spotted several cars and trucks in various stages of rust and decay. Directly in front of them, a decaying building leaned at a forty-five-degree angle. It had been adobe or stucco. It looked as if a good wind would topple it over.

Around the house bushes and plants were brown, wilted, and in various stages of dying. In the distance, he saw trees, not tall, or full, or even green.

Theo stared at something behind him. Alroy followed his gaze. In the distance, green fields and several white-washed adobe buildings stood out in the bleak landscape. Healthy trees provided shade. Horses and cows grazed in a large field. So everything wasn't dying or in a state of decay.

"What is that place, Bella?" Theo asked.

"The Legate Academy, a school of sorts."

"I thought you said this was Southern California?" Theo said. "I'm from Southern California. This isn't right."

"That is the Legate School. And that . . ." Bella pointed in the opposite direction toward rundown buildings and some greenery. "That is Orange Hope."

In the distance, Alroy could make out old buildings, smoke from fires, maybe campfires. Between here and there, vines and other plants grew up around crumbling buildings. He guessed some of the lumps were old cars.

"That's where we were," Lavinia said. "There were three Legates there. Fortinbras, Archangel, and Corday."

"Where is Orange Hope? What part of Southern California? The desert?" Theo looked perplexed as if he couldn't understand what they were seeing.

"South of Los Angeles." Bella pointed in a direction Alroy assumed was North. "Orange Hope is built on the ruins of Newport Beach."

"No. Impossible." Theo took a deep breath. He glanced at Alroy. "I can smell the ocean. Which way is the ocean?"

Bella pointed right. Theo took off running in that direction. Alroy followed him, struggling to keep up. As they ran, Alroy's side burned, but he pushed through to keep up with his friend who was in some kind of shock.

He smelled the fishy smell of the ocean and salt water. The ocean breeze chilled his face. Up ahead Theo slowed to a walk and finally stopped.

When Alroy reached him, he stood on the edge of a sandy bank that inclined toward the sandy beach. The expansive ocean water vanished into the horizon.

The bluish green water rose and fell. Waves crashed on the shore, leaving white foam behind. The beach was littered with debris, not just shells, seaweed, and driftwood, but also other things that looked as if they'd once been manmade. The sun was lower in the sky, moving westward. The shell of a rusting small boat leaned on its side on the beach.

Alroy realized they weren't so much looking at a sandy beach as they were looking at dirt mixed with a little sand. When he finally stood beside Theo, the look on his friend's face shocked him. There were tears in his eyes, but also fear. His already light skin looked pasty.

"Do you need to sit down?"

Theo shook his head. "No. Newport was a beach town, where wealthy people lived. From Los Angeles all the way down the coast to Mexico was like one big city. One city merged with the next city until it seemed like the same place. Millions of people. This . . . I'm not sure what this is." He met Alroy's gaze. "The end of the world. What happened?"

Alroy simply shook his head. "I think Lavinia wants us to see Orange Hope. My friend Toby said it looked like the Wild West. Considering I'm from Los Angeles in the 1890s, that's saying something."

The girls and Bella caught up to them.

"If we walk along the beach, we get to Orange Hope," Lavinia said.

They walked along in silence. Teresa had taken Theo's hand and walked beside him. Lavinia frowned as she walked and didn't make eye contact with Alroy.

"I didn't bring us here to shock you," Lavinia finally said. "After all these years of school, I think I understand what we are trying to do. I think it will help you to see."

No one spoke. The guilt Alroy felt all those years ago returned. He was probably less anxious to see Orange Hope than the others were, but he'd go along because Lavinia had been right about so many things he couldn't dismiss her ideas.

"I will tell you about the Legates as we walk," Bella said.

"Don't leave out our part," Lavinia said.

"How do you know you have a part?"

"An educated guess."

He wanted to tell Bella to listen to Lavinia's educated guesses, but he didn't. The thought he might be involved in something far greater than he realized gripped him. He didn't pay attention when Toby had researched the Legates and rambled on and on about them.

Back then it was gibberish. Now it was relevant.

"The Legates are a group of people from all over the world that are trying to help rebuild civilization after the great disasters that led to the fall of all civilizations. Most of the disasters were natural, some made by human neglect."

Bella paused and glanced out at the ocean. "The Legate schools train children in defense, history, law, government, medicine, cultures, arts . . . all the disciplines. All around the world there are depositories of information vital to restart the fragmented world. Legates are both educated, educators, and fierce warriors who defend those who cannot defend themselves. They establish and help build new communities."

Alroy could see parts of the city up ahead. It looked more like ruins or a ghetto than a town. He stopped and glanced at Lavinia. She figured this out while he'd been worried about passing tests and exercising.

"So," Alroy said. "After the disasters only a few people survived and humans became more violent."

"Yes." Bella nodded. "Three Legates watch over this town, Fortinbras, Corday, and Archangel. They were trained at the Legate Academy behind us. They helped Toby rescue Lavinia, Zella, and Pedro from the local thugs who had captured them."

Theo and Teresa had gone on ahead, but they were close enough to hear their conversation. They both walked back and stopped in front of Bella.

"Do time travelers help create the Legates?" Alroy asked.

"Does the information we gather help them?" Teresa asked.

"When I came here, the Legates were young," Lavinia said. "Like us, only fighters and a little scary. Imagine the worst slums you can. That's Orange Hope. They are proud of it. They have homes, food, and a hospital, while other people are still hunters and gatherers. Other people became bandits, robbers, and pirates, killing and taking what they wanted."

"The portals?" Theo asked.

"When it became evident there was no hope to stop what was happening, the Guardians closed the portals. All time travelers who were left put the Legate program into place."

Bella's voice had softened. Alroy never knew if her human qualities were programmed or if she was evolving into someone with human feelings.

Right now so many conflicting emotions flipped through his mind he didn't know if he could express any of them.

He joined the time travelers because he wanted adventure. He wanted to see the world, to travel, to learn about new cultures. All of that sounded fun, exciting. Now, he realized he and his friends were part of something far greater than he could have imagined before.

They weren't just gathering information for dry history books, or collecting information about building things without technology or how to farm when the weather was extreme. They were compiling information to save the human race and give them the skills to create a better future.

He had a million questions. Couldn't they stop the fall? Could they do something to stop the disasters? Might they somehow change the future? Was their Super Hub part of a grander plan?

They continued walking toward the town. On the ridge above them, a small Asian woman stood with her legs apart and a flail dangling on her belt. A tall, muscular black man frowned at them. He had a red cloth wrapped around his head. A pale slender man with long white hair held up his hand as if telling them to stop.

"The Legates," Bella said.

"Stay back," the black man shouted.

"Fortinbras," Bella said. "I will go up and talk to them."

Theo slowed and walked closer to Alroy. "Let's leave the backpacks with the Legates."

Alroy nodded.

Bella appeared on the hillside beside them. The three stepped back drawing their weapons. Fortinbras held a gun pointed at Bella. The blond man crossed his arms and grinned at the hologram, stepping forward he waved his hand through Bella's image and laughed.

Bella vanished off the hillside and reappeared next to Alroy.

"There is a deadly disease in the town. They were warning us to stay away. Several people have died. They recognized Lavinia. Corday wanted to know if Toby has written more stories."

"Look," Theo said. "I don't know what any of this means, but we are leaving our backpacks. There are a few things there they might need. Could you tell them?"

Bella smiled. "I did already. I heard you and Alroy talking."

Alroy suddenly wanted to see what he was going to

help build. In an instant, he found a mission, something greater than himself and his need for adventure. He could become part of a future legacy.

He wondered if the Legates knew they were making the world a better place. They'd been raised to restart civilization, and he was going to help them.

That was that. Bella opened a portal. They all waved before stepping through to the Super Hub.

Author of *League of the Daring*

CORA FOERSTNER

Advise & Circumvent

Faithful friends lead the way.

Advise & Circumvent

At Woodville StudiosAlone in her dorm room, Lavinia sat at her wide oak desk, writing her thoughts as she brainstormed to clarify her thinking. Somewhere down the hall Janis played her violin, a somber piece that Lavinia didn't know. For some reason the violin relaxed and soothed Lavinia.

After leaving home, she'd become a student of late nineteenth and early twentieth-century history. Her studies led her to music, which led to her appreciation of string instruments.

At first she became engrossed in that era because she wanted to know what she was missing and what her family and friends would experience.

Before coming to the university and studying history, she never worried about the world becoming a horrible place. Now she did. When she left 1891 Los Angeles, she imagined the future as one improvement after another.

Sure, a lot of things had improved. Other things had gotten worse. Not just worse, but slipping backwards instead of moving forward. The contemporary world had serious problems that no one seemed interested in solving.

Studying history, she found out what life had in store for her family and friends. When she went home to visit, she couldn't tell them that their future held two world wars and more.

Now, this day, a kind of desperation she hadn't felt before possessed her. She tried to figure out what her part in saving the world should be or even could be.

She wrote in longhand. It didn't matter how long Lavinia lived in the future, she still preferred paper and fountain pens to computers and word processing. Sure, computers were faster, but putting ink to paper and forming words with her own hands helped her think.

It helped her vague understandings of her life here to solidify.

Two days ago Raymond arrived. With a flick of his hand, he sent Professor Skyles into the past, and helped her, Alroy, and Teresa rescue him.

Now she sat at her desk, a replica of the five-foot oak desk in her father's office, and wrote nonstop. She'd been thinking and writing for two days.

The dim light from the window behind her filtered onto the desk. She realized it was getting darker as dusk settled over the school.

It was nearly time for the evening meal. She needed to put her writing things away. Blue ink stained the knuckle on her middle finger. Her slanted handwriting filled several pages in her journal. At last she leaned back in the wooden chair and sighed.

She realized nothing could have prepared her for the discoveries she'd made. What she realized was that she, Alroy, Theo, and Teresa had a moral obligation to act.

How to proceed? That was the question she needed help answering.

More than anything she wanted to talk to Zella, Toby, and Pedro, her friends and members of the League of the Daring, living back in 1896.

Going home without a reason or permission wasn't allowed. She was tempted to do it anyway. Alroy would join her. She didn't doubt that, but was it right to ask him?

All the students came here for different reasons. She came because she wanted to learn about the new scientific discoveries and become a better scientist.

Alroy wanted adventure. While some students might try to hide that simple desire by spouting lofty ideas, he didn't. He wanted to travel and experience everything. She admired him for his honesty.

Teresa loved history and dreamed of cataloging events and making discoveries about yet unknown gaps in history. She loved history from ordinary people's points of view.

Once when Richard was a little tipsy, he told Lavinia that he wanted to travel back in time to make sure his grandparents never met. That would erase him from history. He didn't care because both his grandparents and his parents were monsters.

She didn't tell him that might just create a separate timeline. His monstrous relations would still be in this timeline. He still would have to face his unpleasant reality.

She worried about him and didn't always trust him to have her back when they traveled.

Right now none of that mattered. She needed real, honest confirmation about what time travelers were actually doing. It was one thing to think she was right. It was another to confirm it. She wanted facts before acting.

Lavinia scrubbed her hands. She went to the cafeteria with faded blue ink on her fingers. The chatter and laughter coming from the dining room sounded pleasant. She stood in the doorway and scanned the tables, searching for Alroy.

The mammoth room with its white walls and black and white floors always made her shiver. A cold and uninviting atmosphere didn't promote digestion.

Sometimes she wished they had a small dining room. Now that most of them were graduating, dining together in a homey environment didn't seem to matter as much as previously.

The smell of roasted chicken filled the air and overpowered whatever vegetables and other food were on the menu. She glanced around again.

At a table near the long windows at the back, a hand went up and waved. Teresa, her brown hair up in a ponytail, smiled as she waved.

Lavinia strolled toward the back, passing a table with four teachers still eating. Professor Hastings' brown eyes narrowed and glared at her as she passed the teachers' table. She knew the woman blamed her and Alroy for Professor Skyles' injuries, never mind that a Guardian had sent him back to Nazi Germany.

Holding her head high, she ignored Hastings and the

other teachers. She hurried to the back toward Teresa's table.

Thankfully, the other students ignored her. Either they didn't care about the rumors or they thought they were false. Anyway, that's what she hoped.

2

She slid into the empty chair beside Teresa. "Have you seen Alroy?"

Teresa pointed toward the door with her chin. Alroy had stopped in the wide opening and glanced around. Lavinia waved and watched as he passed the teachers' table. He received the same stares as she had gotten.

A sinking feeling that they were in trouble with all the teachers punched her in the stomach. If she followed her newly formed plan, she'd be in even more trouble.

Teresa passed her a plate of roasted chicken. Without thinking, Lavinia scooped a slice onto her plate, grabbed mashed potatoes, and poured a tall glass of water.

Alroy took the seat next to her. He'd been avoiding sitting next to Teresa, who seemed to be getting his message without any kind of confrontation.

That was Alroy's style and not particularly nice of him. Ignoring the girl and letting her figure out that he wasn't interested seemed like the coward's way.

"Professor Skyles is better. He seemed chipper when I spoke to him." Alroy filled his plate as he spoke.

"What's the answer to the big question?" Teresa asked.

He finished chewing. "Which question is that?"

"Is he angry with us?" Teresa glanced toward the

teachers' table, which was empty except for Hastings, who continued to scowl at them.

Alroy nodded, which wasn't exactly an answer.

"No," he whispered. "I think he's scared. Scared of Raymond. Scared of traveling. Scared that they aren't training us properly."

"Good." Lavinia watched Hastings carry her tray to the side of the room where everyone stacked their dishes.

When Hastings vanished into the hallway, Alroy leaned forward and put his elbows on the table and his fingers intertwined. He sighed.

"Several of the teachers want to expel us from the program. Skyles is trying to talk them down. He's obsessed with revising the curriculum. We were the only ones who had trouble with the exams. We were the only ones who took action." Alroy shook his head.

"Maybe that's why Raymond did what he did?" Teresa said.

"You mean to show Skyles how dangerous time travel can be?" Alroy asked.

Teresa grabbed a fresh baked roll and slid it into her pocket. She nodded.

"I've been thinking the same thing," Lavinia whispered. "The older travelers stopped traveling years ago. They were young back when they traveled. I think we might have more current experience than they do."

Teresa stood. "I have to go, but I want to know everything you talk about when I'm gone."

Lavinia watched Teresa's progress across the room. There were two other students at a table near the door. She turned back to Alroy.

"We have to go home," she and Alroy spoke at once.

She leaned back in her chair and nodded. "Why do you want to go home?"

"Do you know anyone else who gives better advice than Toby? Or Zella?"

"Or Pedro, Wyatt, and Ernest?" She chuckled. "You don't know how many times I've wished they were here with us. Well, maybe not Wyatt."

"I've decided Wyatt's okay. I've been bullheaded about him for years. Too bad. I've missed out on being close to my brother. What about you? Why go home?"

"I think we need to do something about the curriculum. Skyles is already there. Getting the other teachers there will take time. My biggest concern is the future. We can't ignore what we found in the basement. Did you tell Skyles?"

Alroy shook his head.

"That's what I want advice about. You know Raymond. He pokes people but never tells us what to do," Lavinia said.

Alroy took another big scoop of mashed potatoes and a chicken leg.

"I think we got huge nudges. First Skyles' rescue and then the Super Hub under us. I know it sounds crazy, but I think Raymond wants us to do something about these things."

She grimaced. Did Raymond think they were his troublemakers? Did he expect them to stir things up? Those questions annoyed her, but truthfully, she didn't mind being a troublemaker if that got things done.

"Those are the exact things I want to talk about," she

said. "I've been brainstorming for two days. I don't know what's right. Will Skyles let us go home?"

Alroy frowned. "No. But we have to go. We have to tell Grace and the others about the Super Hub. I've been wondering if one or more of the teachers knowns about the Hub and is using it for something."

"Like helping the rogue time travelers?"

Lavinia didn't like to think about the rogue travelers they'd helped capture. Their goal had been to take over all the dimensions and rule them as overlords. She knew they wouldn't be like the Guardians whose goals were research.

"I hadn't thought of that," Alroy said. "I thought the teachers might panic when they found out about the Hub. But wouldn't Raymond tell DIT about the Super Hub?"

"No. In his mind that would be interfering." She glanced around the room.

"So, we leave tonight."

"Can't. As soon as we step through the portal, the teachers will know we've left," Lavinia stood up. "Let's get out of here."

Alroy took her arm and tugged her downward. She sat.

"We use the Super Hub," Alroy whispered. "Bella said she'd get us home and back moments after we left. Bella sent Toby a message. The others will meet us in the attic."

The attic at Alroy's home was the League of the Daring's meeting place. She had great memories of their times together. The attic was a hodgepodge of old furniture, worktables for their projects, and a haven away from adults who always wanted to mold them into proper people. It had been at least two years since they'd all been there together.

People always accused Lavinia of being pushy. She didn't disagree. She got things done. Were her habits rubbing off on Alroy? Actually, she hoped so. Sometimes he was too congenial.

"All right. Anyway we do it, we will get caught. DIT needs to know about the Hub. And, there's the whole end of the world future we have to discuss with sane people."

"Yeah. Do we tell anyone else? Teresa?"

"She should know. But if we tell her ahead of time, she could get into as much trouble as we do. Tell her when we get back?"

Alroy nodded.

3

Two hours later, Lavinia stepped through the portal that Bella opened. Alroy followed her. It was dark inside the attic. Moonlight filtered through the window. Lavinia knew the room well enough that she moved forward and turned on the lights.

Alroy stood next to the portal waiting for her to turn on the lights. When she glanced back, he stood gaping and glancing around the attic.

The first things she noticed were new window curtains. They were still lacy, but not the worn ones they'd repaired over the years.

A large new wool carpet with pink roses on a tan background covered the floor from the attic's entrance to the window that faced the street. This was new and attractive.

Squinting at the furniture, she realized it was the same old discarded pieces of furniture they'd collected over the years. But now, it looked new. Her friends had reupholstered the chairs, love seat, and even put matching cushions on the wooden desk chairs.

The small sofa had been lumpy and so uncomfortable that League of the Daring members raced each other for the better overstuffed chairs. The solid green fabric blended with the carpet. Even the arrangement of the sofa and chairs looked grown-up.

This had to be Zella's handy work. No, she corrected herself. Toby helped her. There were three matching mahogany desks.

A little nip of sadness and jealousy grew in her chest. The long, well sanded and varnished work table at the back of the room held a model expansion bridge. It had to be Pedro's work.

She realized she'd expected things here to stay static. Toby, Zella, and Pedro had moved forward.

She saw her friends three or four times a year for short visits. But they hadn't used the attic as a meeting place in years.

Knowing things had changed and that her friends had a life separate from her own hit home like a violent tempest. She thought of herself as sophisticated and her friends as simple. She'd made the same mistake many of the students at TTU had made about her and other students from the past.

Before she or Alroy had time to speak, the sound of

footsteps on the stairs drew her attention away from the changes to the door that flew open. Zella squealed and rushed forward, throwing her arms around Lavinia and then rushing to Alroy.

Toby stood in the doorway grinning and watching. He was taller than she remembered and fit like the men in the magazines the girls in the dorm liked to read. His wild brown hair was combed back. He looked like a dapper young man who'd stepped out of the pages of a history book.

The men from this time dressed more formally. Toby's black suit had a vest that was nothing like the casual suits he wore in the past. He winked at her and came forward to hug her.

The same as always, sweet and casual. As he moved toward Alroy, Pedro stepped into the room. Her heart did one thump and settled. She guessed she'd always feel a little guilty that she'd moved on so quickly from their romance.

Back in high school, Toby had what she thought was a dumb theory. He always explained that most high school romances didn't last. It was natural. She guessed he'd been right.

Pedro's handsome face had grown more mature, manly. And more handsome. He said hello, but didn't hug her. She knew he was trying to make her comfortable, but his reluctance made her more aware of the awkwardness between them.

Plus, she wasn't going to take a smile and a nod from one of her best friends. She went to him, her arms outstretched. That hug removed the tension. His shoulders visibly relaxed.

She realized they hadn't been home in a year. She and Alroy had just burst into their lives without warning. Everyone talked excitedly, and she couldn't follow any of the conversations. This was the first time she felt out of place here.

Zella's red hair was swept up in an attractive hairdo that framed her face. Lavinia envied her pale green dress. Her T-shirt and jeans looked shabby by comparison. She didn't think she'd miss dressing in long dresses, surrounded by volumes of fabric. But she did.

Zella grabbed her hand and pulled her closer. "Why are you so quiet?"

"I'm shocked. The attic has changed. You are so grown-up." She glanced at the boys who were gathered around Pedro's bridge as he explained his plan. "Toby is surprisingly handsome," she whispered.

"Whatever you do, don't tell him. He has women throwing themselves at him. It's quite annoying. He has somehow managed not to become too arrogant. Come, let's talk."

Zella pulled her toward the sofa, where they sat in comfort.

"Who did all this?"

"Toby and I. Well, my mother helped. We all work here. Toby runs his publishing company from here. I write articles for the *Herald* and a few magazines. I haven't told you, but I'm also writing novels for Toby. I have a series about Jane Roberts, Woman Detective."

"Wonderful." Lavinia hoped it was wonderful. She had

a feeling her friends were growing closer while she and Alroy were becoming more and more out of step with them.

She grinned before continuing her recitation. "Toby's idea about the books. At first he had to force me to add in a little romance. Now I throw it in every book. Tell me about school. Are you finished? We were surprised to get Bella's message."

Lavinia sat up a little straighter and glanced at Alroy and made eye contact. He turned back to Toby and Pedro and whispered something.

"We came to talk to you three. Technically, we left without telling anyone. We are probably in trouble, and we need advice."

4

They sat on the new furniture as Lavinia and Alroy took turns explaining what Raymond did to Professor Skyles, the Super Hub they found in the school's basement, and the disastrous events that brought about the destruction of people worldwide.

Some of the problems like wars and climate change they probably shouldn't have told them about, but Lavinia didn't care. She knew they'd keep that knowledge to themselves.

While they talked, Pedro leaned forward, listening intently. In typical Zella form, she took notes, while Toby sat back, casual but listening.

To an outsider, Toby appeared indifferent as if he were thinking about something else. Lavinia knew he was listening because he'd been acting as if nothing bothered him since she could remember.

Alroy had a daunting task of trying to explain the terrible circumstances of Nazi Germany without giving away too much history. So he bumbled through his explanation of the rescue of Skyles.

Watching Pedro's facial expression go from curiosity to incredulity and to outright confusion revealed how crazy Alroy's explanation sounded to people in 1896.

When Alroy finished, Toby cleared his throat and shook his head.

"To summarize, Alroy was just sounding crazy because he's trying not to tell us about the near future. Right?"

"Yes." Alroy sighed and leaned back in his chair. "That was exhausting."

"And made no sense," Zella added.

Pedro stood and walked to the window. His arms folded over his chest, he stood there for a few seconds in the quiet room. Lavinia wanted to say something, but she was afraid she'd make things worse.

When Pedro turned back to the group, he spoke softly. "Toby, can you summarize?"

"I see three major issues. First, Raymond. He shows up, causes a serious problem by sending a teacher into the danger zone of Germany in the 1940 something." Toby paused. "We all know Raymond shows up when he wants to change something. He pretends he's not interfering, but he does by causing trouble that the time travelers have to fix."

"Yes, exactly," Alroy said.

"So, you two and your friend rescued the good professor, which is forcing the school to reexamine their teaching system. It hasn't trained students to deal with problems and issues that come up. Especially dangerous problems." Toby raised his eyebrows and waited.

Lavinia nodded.

"Second, you went to the end of the world, which we already knew about because—"

"Yes, because of me." Alroy grinned.

"What we didn't know is that the time travelers started the Legates. Time travelers collected information to help survivors restart civilization. The problem is time travelers aren't doing that. It's urgent they start the program."

"Yes," Lavinia said. "I think we somehow need to jumpstart this. Helping people in the future makes time travel seem urgent."

"Or, lets things happen as they naturally would and people will rebuild," Pedro said.

"Yes, maybe that will work, but . . . ." Alroy shrugged.

"But if we know, shouldn't we do something to help?" Zella grinned. "You know evil triumphs when good men do nothing."

Everyone chuckled. Burke's quotation hung over their door until Lavinia came back from TTU and informed them that Burke may not have ever said such a thing. They all agreed that it didn't matter if he said it because it was true.

Toby nodded and continued with his summary.

"Last, your Super Hub problem. That one's easy. We need to go talk to Grace. Connect the Hub problem with the school being hidden away and the students isolated. When we talk to Grace, you need to argue for your desire to be part of the world. I'd focus on how the teachers are isolated and don't see the serious problems around them."

"Just talking to Grace isn't going to solve everything. She doesn't run the school or make its rules," Lavinia said.

"So, maybe suggest a board of directors to create guidelines for the school," Zella said.

"Maybe Otis, Mr. Lee, and a couple other experienced travelers. I think the Legate Program should be a major part of time travelers' mission statement." Pedro grinned. "They are old, but practical. Especially Mr. Lee."

Toby stood. "Let's get Wyatt and Ernest onboard and rope Otis and Mr. Lee into our plan. Then we all go to DIT."

"None of this will be easy," Lavinia said. "Maybe impossible. Grace won't go for it."

Grace was their friend, a time traveler who chose to live in this time. For one moment Lavinia thought she understood why Grace stayed here rather than in a more progressive future. Maybe she was trying to prevent some of the problems before they started. She remembered Grace's ongoing debate with Grimes, a scientist who wanted to promote gas vehicles.

"I take that back," Lavinia said. "I think Grace will listen to us."

The thing she never said aloud was that the school needed a strong leader. Professor Skyles was a great person, but not a strong leader.

As far as she could tell, the university teachers made up the rules and regulations as they went along. She wondered if there was any kind of organized structure for the students who were graduating to begin their career in time travel.

As much as she still had these worries and fears, Toby and the others had confirmed what she already knew. They had to bypass the professors and risk annoying Grace and the other DIT leaders.

The gears of the dumbwaiter began turning. The sounds grew louder as whatever was being sent up got closer. Lavinia knew that Liza, the Doyle family's friend and cook, who loved to feed people, was sending a meal up.

The smell of roast beef and potatoes reached them first.

"I smell apple pie." Toby grinned. "Bless Liza."

They put aside their discussion and feasted on Liza's dinner. Lavinia and Alroy didn't tell them they'd already eaten. Then they talked strategy into the early morning hours.

4

The next day, they went to Wyatt, Ernest, Otis, and Mr. Lee and convinced them to support their quest.

And that was how, less than twenty-four hours after they'd arrived in 1896, they sat at the long conference table in DIT's headquarters somewhere in space and waited for Grace to arrive.

The table, like most tables in the Hub, was clear, like plastic, but not plastic or glass or anything else in their human culture. Lavinia lay her hand on the smooth, cool, vibrating material. For the first time, she made the connection between the vibrating of the portals and the vibrations of Guardian tech.

Grace's curly brown hair hung down around her shoulders and looked as if she'd run through a wind storm as she walked into the room with Raymond. Behind them Professor Skyles hobbled into the room using a cane.

The professor smiled at Lavinia, which didn't do much to relieve her stomach muscles, which were so tense she wasn't sure if she'd ever be able to eat again. She hadn't planned on him being here, but it was probably better.

The room at least wasn't bland and bare. Someone had decorated the walls with pictures from every century and country in their dimension. There was a blue and gray rug on the floor. Plus a very large glass vase filled with a dozen different long stemmed flowers sat in the center of the table.

The smell of roses and lavender filled the room, reminding Lavinia of summer picnics in her backyard.

Lavinia took a deep breath and slowly glanced around the table. Her grandparents, Otis and Martha, and Mr. Lee, another old time traveler, sat near the head of the table where Grace, Raymond, and Profess Skyles took their seats.

Wyatt and Ernest sat with the League of the Daring. Somewhere in the League of the Daring's adventures, Wyatt, Alroy's brother, and Ernest, Grace's brother and Wyatt's best friend, had become part of the League of the Daring.

Lavinia realized the League lost her and Alroy but gained Wyatt and Ernest.

Lavinia didn't protest being called a member of the League. For her that was the beginning of everything good in her life. She felt surprisingly comfortable surrounded by her friends.

As they'd agreed, Ernest stood and systematically presented their ideas. When he reached the part about a Super Hub under the university, Grace and the professor started and glanced at each other.

Ernest continued talking seemingly unaware of the surprised responses. Lavinia thought perhaps they'd made a mistake not telling Professor Skyles about the Super Hub, but there wasn't anything they could do about that now.

When Ernest finished speaking, an uncomfortable silence settled over the room. Grace glanced around and her gaze finally stopped on the professor.

"Did you know about this Super Hub?"

"This is the first I'm hearing of it."

Grace squinted at Raymond before turning her anger toward Lavinia. "How long have you known about this?"

"Two days."

Ernest, a lawyer, warned Lavinia and the others to answer with yes or no and short answers if more was required. She was determined to follow his advice.

"Why didn't you inform Professor Skyles immediately?"

"He was in the infirmary with broken bones." Lavinia glanced at Alroy.

"If I may speak," the professor said and waited for Grace's nod. "The other teachers are intimidated by

Lavinia and Alroy. I think because they have more time travel experience than most of us."

The professor glanced at Raymond before continuing. "When Guardian Raymond sent me back in time, frankly, I was terrified. I was tortured."

He raised a hand as if quieting a room full of students who were not talking.

"It was the best thing that could have happened to me. I would rather not have been injured. But the experience helped me realize the university hasn't been preparing the students for real time travel."

Grace frowned and glared at Raymond. "Why did you send him back in time?"

"I've been monitoring the university and had some concerns. I sent him back as a sort of lesson about time travel."

"You could have come to me." Grace hadn't taken her eyes off Raymond.

He shrugged. "I could have, but Skyles wouldn't have understood the problem or how to solve it."

Since the professor said as much himself, Grace didn't continue her questioning. She did go around the table and ask every person there if they agreed with the problems as they were presented.

The first thing that surprised Lavinia was that Raymond freely admitted that he tossed the professor into the Nazi's hands to get their attention. Second, everyone at the table agreed with the problems, including the university being held in space and the need for a physical location in real time.

Secretly Lavinia wanted to shout because that also

meant that their time travel headquarters would also be in a physical location. In the end, the group agreed on everything. Not willing to rock the boat, Lavinia didn't ask if they were kicked out of Time Travel University.

But apparently Ernest didn't have any qualms about asking. Professor Skyles immediately answered.

"No, they are not kicked out of the university. My hope is they will stick around to help us iron out all the details of what needs to be done and help us find a location for the university and the headquarters. I require one thing. Do not mention these things or this meeting until I've discussed everything with the other teachers."

Lavinia was relieved about everything except for the sticking around part of his little speech. Neither she nor Alroy said they wanted to be involved with starting the Legate Program, but they did want to be part of setting things up. She didn't really think that would happen. She thought Grace and the others would give the old timers control.

Grace stood to leave. She gathered up her notes and then her gaze turned to the end of the table where the League of the Daring sat.

"You all realize that you are emerging as time travel leaders. Someday, one of you will be standing in my shoes or Professor Skyles' shoes, or Otis' and Mr. Lee's shoes. Proceed with care."

She turned and left. The League of the Daring stared after her. Lavinia glanced at Alroy, whose face seemed to say, "You, not me." She wanted to say aloud. "Toby, if any of us."

5

They spent the next two days with their families and returned to the Super Hub a few seconds after they left.

Bella, her hair bright blue and in two pony tails waited for them at the portal.

For the first time in weeks, Lavinia was looking forward to what would happen next. Professor Skyles and Grace both agreed that she and Alroy could be founding members of the Legate Program. She wondered how many teachers that would annoy. Probably all of them.

She didn't care. They now had a clear purpose and something she could throw all her energies into completing.

Things were turning out very differently from what she'd expected five years ago when she and Alroy first came to the university.

Need More Time Travel Stories?

If you enjoyed these stories, check out Cora Foerstner's *League of the Daring series*: see where Alroy and Lavinia's time travel journey began.

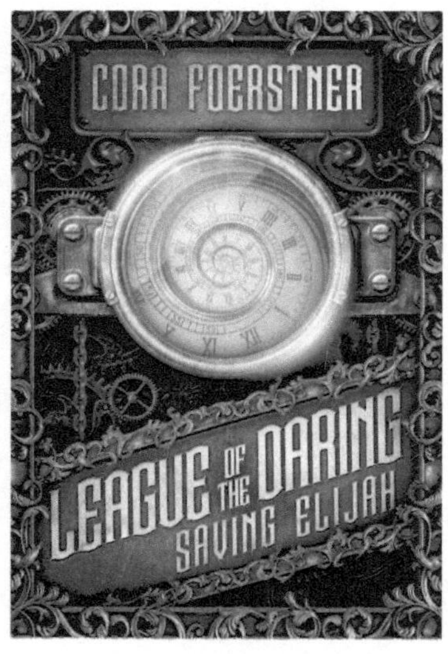
CORA FOERSTNER
LEAGUE OF THE DARING
SAVING ELIJAH

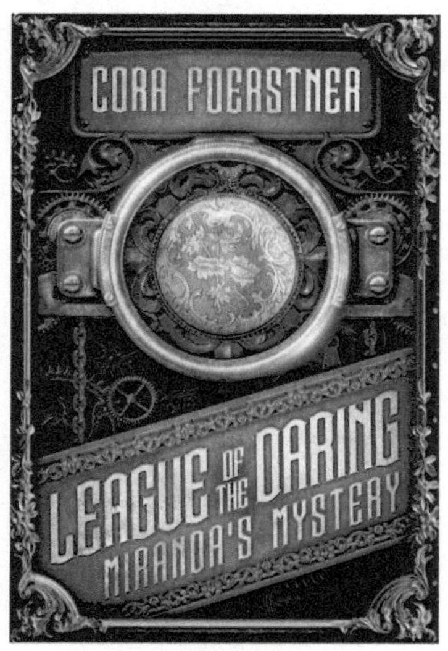
CORA FOERSTNER
LEAGUE OF THE DARING
MIRANDA'S MYSTERY

Also by Cora Foerstner

The Dragon Speakers: an epic fantasy duology.

Dragon Speakers

Defying the King

The League of the Daring: a alternate history, time travel, mystery series.

Finding Pedro (League of the Daring #1)

Saving Elijah (League of the Daring #2)

Miranda's Mystery (League of the Daring #3)

Short story Collections:

Christmas Magic: 5 Original Holiday Shorts Stories

Have Portal. Will Travel: 5 Original Short Stories set in the League of the Daring World.

Coming Soon:

Swords for Hire: a fantasy adventure series set in the Dragon Speakers World. It takes place seventy years after *Defying the King.*

Results Unknown (Swords for Hire #1)

Results Hazy (Swords for Hire #2)

Results Pending (Swords for Hire #3)

Results Baffling (Swords for Hire #4)

By direct from Cora at www.woodsorrelstudios.com. Her books are available at all major online outlets; use this link to find her

books at your preferred store: https://books2read.com/
corafoerstner/

About Cora Foerstner

Cora Foerstner wanted to be a spy when she was a teenager. Danger, adventure, and exotic places sounded amazing. Since that life didn't pan out, she figured the next best thing would be to tell stories about adventure, danger, mysteries, awesome places, and people she wished were real.

When Cora isn't writing science fiction and fantasy stories, she plays video games, drinks lots of coffee and green tea, and researches things like dragons, climate change, the end of the world, and other unsavory subjects. She is a super fangirl of the Expanse Series (Books & TV). She never misses a superhero movie.

facebook.com/CoraLFoerstner

instagram.com/corafoerstner

goodreads.com/corafoerstner

amazon.com/author/corafoerstner

bookbub.com/profile/cora-foerstner

www.ingramcontent.com/pod-product-compliance
Lightning Source LLC
Chambersburg PA
CBHW021717190726
48289CB00008B/2581